WARPED GALAXIES

CLAWS OF THE

GENESTEALER

WARHAMMER ADVENTURES

STORIES FROM THE FAR FUTURE

WARPED GALAXIES

WARHAMMER ADVENTURES

STORIES IN AN AGE OF FANTASY

REALM QUEST

WARPED GALAXIES

CLAWS OF THE

GENESTEALER

CAVAN SCOTT

WARHAMMER ADVENTURES

First published in Great Britain in 2019 by
Warhammer Publishing,
Willow Road,
Nottingham, NG7 2WS, UK.

10 9 8 7 6 5 4 3 2 1

Produced by Games Workshop in Nottingham.
Cover illustration by Cole Marchetti.
Internal illustrations by Magnus Norén & Cole Marchetti.

A CIP record for this book is available from the British Library.

ISBN 13: 978 1 78496 781 9

See Warhammer Adventures on the internet at

warhammeradventures.com

Find out more about Games Workshop and the worlds of
Warhammer 40,000 and Warhammer Age of Sigmar at

games-workshop.com

Printed and bound by CPI Group (UK) Ltd, Croydon, CR0 4YY

For Tom.

Contents

The Imperium
of the Far Future

Life in the 41st millennium is hard.
Ruled by the Emperor of Mankind
from his Golden Throne on Terra,
humans have spread across the
galaxy, inhabiting millions of planets.
They have achieved so much, from
space travel to robotics, and yet
billions live in fear. The universe
seems a dangerous place, teeming
with alien horrors and dark powers.
But it is also a place bristling with
adventure and wonder, where battles
are won and heroes are forged.

CHAPTER ONE

The Hunt

The forest was silent. A fresh blanket of snow had fallen overnight, drifting through the gaps of the strange mushroom-trees. No birds whirled above their wide, frozen caps, nor were there insects crawling along their mottled stalks.

Heat had no place here. At night anyone caught outside without protection would freeze, and conditions barely improved during the day.

A snout pushed out of the snow. A small, pot-bellied creature scrabbled from its burrow. The tiny ridge-boar, barely a month old, shook snow from its milk-white spines. It snorted, its breath misting in front of stubby tusks. The boarlet looked around, its eyes becoming accustomed to the glare of the surface. It lifted its blunt nose into the chilly air and sniffed once... twice...

Satisfied that no predators lay in wait, the young creature trotted deeper into the forest. It didn't care about the snow, or the tracks it left in its wake. All it cared about was the gnawing hunger in its belly.

It struggled on, the trot becoming a scramble, the boar's skinny legs disappearing into the snowdrift. Every now and then it stopped, churning up the snow with its snout, searching in vain for roots or berries. The snow was too thick, the ground too hard.

Its nose twitched. There was a scent, something new. The boar darted forwards. There, in the middle of a clearing, a pile of dried flakes lay piled on a stump. The boar crept towards them cautiously, sniffing the air.

The smell of the food made its belly rumble. The animal pounced upon the unexpected feast, grinding the flakes between its teeth. They tasted so good.

Unfortunately, they were also a trap.

A net flashed through the air. The ridge-boar squealed, kicking up snow as it scampered away. The net missed its target, landing on the stump. The boar disappeared between the frozen stalks, and a nearby voice cursed.

Talen Stormweaver stepped out from his hiding place and grunted in frustration. He had been so close that time. If only he'd been quicker springing the trap. With a sigh, he snatched up the net he'd woven from voidship cables, shaking loose the excess snow. At least the hunt hadn't been a complete waste of time, not like yesterday or the day before. This time he'd actually found something. This time he had tracks to follow.

Trying to tread quietly, Talen followed the hoof-marks in the snow. Two weeks

they'd been on this Throne-forsaken
planet. Two weeks. He still wasn't used
to the cold. Yes, he was wrapped in
a thick thermo-coat, but the chill was
relentless. He'd almost forgotten what it
was like to be warm.

Talen wasn't used to this. Home
was the tunnels beneath Rhal Rata,
the largest hive on Targian. It was
never cold beneath the great city. It
was wet and dark and stank so bad
your eyes watered, but you were never
in danger of freezing to death. You
could be attacked by another gang or
find yourself facing dire-cats in the
crawlways, but you were always warm.
Plus, food was everywhere, even if most
of it didn't belong to you. There were
stalls ripe for looting in the markets
above and plump sewer rats fresh for
hunting in the tunnels below.

Here, there was nothing.

No, that wasn't exactly true. There
was a ridge-boar. He just had to find it
again.

Of course, his home wasn't there any more.

There had been times when he'd loathed life on Targian, but now the planet was gone forever. The entire hive world had been torn apart by the Necrons, living alien machines. Talen had escaped the destruction, more by luck than by judgement, and had ended up on this ice-box with a ragtag bunch of survivors. There was Erasmus, a stuffy old lexmechanic, and Zelia, one of the bossiest girls he'd ever met. They were the normal ones. The rest of the group was made up of Mekki, a Martian kid who was happier dealing with machines than humans, Fleapit, an orange-furred Jokaero with a knack of making weapons out of next to nothing, and a tiny winged robot called a servo-sprite. It was Fleapit who had fashioned their thermo-coats, and who had somehow transformed their cramped escape pod into a shelter large enough to house all six of them.

No, Talen corrected himself. Not six. Not any more.

A Necron Hunter had followed them to the ice planet, searching for an ancient artefact the old man had been hiding – the Diadem. They had barely survived with their lives, and only because Erasmus had made the ultimate sacrifice. The archeotech had lured the Hunter into the path of an avalanche. Both were buried beneath tonnes of snow on the other side of the mountain.

At least, they *hoped* the Hunter was buried. Talen had seen those skeletal horrors in action, seen them repair themselves in the heat of battle. They could also leap from place to place, phasing in and out of real space. Every night, Talen dreamed of steel skeletons clawing their way out of icy tombs, or appearing above his bed, green eyes blazing.

Zelia told him he was being paranoid. 'The fact that we're still breathing

proves that it's destroyed,' she'd told
him, 'or at least damaged beyond repair.
It's gone. We're safe.'

The Diadem itself was now stashed in
Mekki's backpack, shielded by a gizmo
that the Martian had made from a
vox-caster. It would stop other Necrons
from finding it, at least that's what
Zelia said.

Zelia said a lot of things. She and
the others were content to sit in the
shelter, huddled near the distress
beacon Mekki and Fleapit had erected,
waiting to be rescued. Not Talen. The
escape pod's emergency rations were
almost exhausted. Someone had to find
more food, and it might as well be him.

Besides, no one was coming to help.
The beacon had pulsed for two weeks
with no answer. It was time to face
facts. They were stranded.

Talen crept through the towering
stalks, wincing as his boots crunched in
the snow. He didn't want to scare the
animal any more than he already had.

There it was, floundering in the snow ahead. The boar was caught in some kind of root, unable to get away. The more it thrashed, the more entangled it became. Finally, a stroke of luck!

Talen grinned. 'Hello, lunch!'

Talen rushed forwards, throwing his home-made net over the creature. The boar squealed, extending its spines to protect itself.

'Shut up, will you?' Talen complained as he pulled the net tight, the boar trussed safely inside. It writhed and screamed but had no way to escape. 'How can something so small make so much noise?'

There was another snort, over to his left. Talen looked and saw a second ridge-boar glaring at him. While the one in his net was an infant, this one was fully grown, spikes bristling along its arched back. It glared at Talen, head down, large pointed tusks jutting forwards.

'Nice piggy,' said Talen, raising what

he hoped was a calming hand. 'Nothing to see here. Go on. Shoo.'

With a ferocious bellow, the angry boar charged straight for him. Talen let go of the net and ran for his life.

'Help!' he screamed, although no one could hear him. The boar was almost on him, grunting as it carved a path through the snow.

Talen's muscles burned with the effort of running through the thick snow. He pelted forwards, and then cried out in alarm as the ground disappeared beneath him.

He fell, tumbling through thin air, before landing with a bone-jarring crunch far below. Snow tumbled down from above. The boar had stopped itself from following Talen over the edge. It snuffled around the hole that had opened beneath his feet. Talen groaned, clutching his arm as the animal gave up on its revenge and scooted away.

Talen tried to sit up, and pain lanced through his shoulder. He couldn't move his arm. Was it broken?

Breathing hard, he looked around at his new surroundings. Icy walls rose high on either side of him. He had no hope of climbing them with one arm. He pushed himself up to a sitting position, trying not to pass out with the pain, and stared into the gloom of the cave. Were those passages in the shadows? Had he tumbled into a labyrinth? He was used to navigating tunnels, but at least he had known

where he was going back on Targian. He had no way of knowing where these icy passages led. One false move and he could stumble into an even bigger drop.

Grimacing, he reached into his coat, searching for his vox. Fleapit had fashioned small communicators for each of them, and Talen prayed that his hadn't been damaged in the fall. He pulled it out of his vest. The case was cracked, but hopefully it would still work.

'Hello?' he croaked, opening a channel. 'Can you hear me? Zelia? Mekki? Anyone?'

There was no answer. He shook the box and tried again. Someone would answer, sooner or later.

They just had to...

CHAPTER TWO

Into the Pit

'Where have you got to, Talen?'

Zelia peered through her omniscope, searching the line of mushroom-trees that formed the edge of the forest. The ganger was nowhere to be seen. The minute Talen had told her about his hunting expedition, Zelia had known it was a bad idea. She'd begged him not to head out alone, and yet he'd gone anyway. It was bad enough that they'd lost Erasmus, she didn't want to lose Talen as well.

She dropped the omniscope from her eye, the thought of Erasmus bringing a fresh pang of grief. He'd been the one who had got them into this mess, keeping his Necron artefact secret, but had paid a terrible price to protect them. He was one of her mum's oldest friends. How on Terra was Zelia going to break the news when they finally got off this planet?

But that was a concern for another day. Right now, she needed to find Talen. By the look of the heavy clouds in the sky, a storm was coming in fast. They'd been here long enough to learn the signs. Talen should have known better.

She trudged back through the series of posts that ringed the camp, flicking a switch on her jacket sleeve to activate Fleapit's sonic fence. A wall of sound hummed into life behind her. While it wouldn't stop a Necron, it would make life uncomfortable for any wild animals that were tempted to investigate their temporary home.

A large, snow-flecked dome sat in the middle of the camp. It had started life as their escape pod from the *Mercator*, but Fleapit had worked his techno-magic. The resulting shelter was now somehow three times the pod's original size. Mekki sat at the door which had once been the lifeboat's airlock, tapping the small screen he wore cuffed to his left arm. The Martian's other arm was withered, the result of an illness when he was a baby back on the Red Planet. He wore a brass exo-frame of his own design around the affected limb that was permanently connected to both the large backpack he wore and the shimmering electoos on his pale skin.

'Where's Fleapit?' she asked as she approached the hatch. The ape-like Jokaero was nowhere to be seen, nor was Mekki's servo-sprite, a tiny robotic imp that kept everything working.

Mekki shrugged, not looking up from his screen. 'I do not know. Perhaps Flegan-Pala has gone on another scavenging run,' he said, using Fleapit's full name, as was his custom. 'I have not seen him for hours.'

'Not him as well,' Zelia sighed, looking over at a smaller tent not far from the main dome. That was Fleapit's own private nest. Zelia hoped that the Jokaero was safely holed up in it, rather than tramping off in the snow somewhere. The bad-tempered alien had soon decided that living alongside humans wasn't for him, no matter how well he seemed to get on with Mekki.

She had to admit being a little jealous of their relationship. Mekki and

Fleapit had bonded over building the distress beacon. She hadn't minded at first. She and Talen had been getting on fine, but as the days had stretched into weeks, Talen had become moody and argumentative, not used to being told what to do. That didn't mean she didn't want him back in camp now. He'd freeze if he was still out there when the blizzard hit.

'Any luck?' she asked Mekki as she approached the hatch.

'He is not responding to messages.'

'And you can't locate his vox-box?'

Mekki shook his head. Zelia sighed, trying to rub some warmth back into her arms. 'He has to be somewhere.'

The snow crunched behind her. She turned, hoping to see Talen, but it was only Fleapit, deactivating the sonic fence as he and the servo-sprite re-entered the camp.

'Where have you been?' she asked as the hairy alien lolloped towards them, the sprite flitting around his head on fragile mesh wings. 'Did you see Talen?'

The Jokaero ignored her, heading straight for Mekki. She tried not to bristle at the snub. The Martian was the only one of them who could understand Fleapit, the two of them communicating by some kind of electronic telepathy.

'No,' Mekki said, answering a seemingly silent question. 'He has been gone since dawn.'

The Jokaero grunted and pulled Mekki's wrist-screen towards him. The alien's long fingers tapped the display, reprogramming the device, before letting go of the boy's arm.

A voice hissed out of the screen's vox. *'Hello? Can anyone hear me?'*

'That's him,' Zelia said. 'That's Talen.'

She tapped her own vox, stitched into her jacket's sleeve. 'We hear you, Talen. Where are you?'

'Where am I? Where were you?' came his reply. *'I've been calling for ages.'*

'Flegan-Pala had to boost the signal,'

Mekki explained. 'There is a lot of interference.'

'That'll be the cave walls. They look pretty thick.'

Zelia frowned. 'What cave?'

'I fell into a sinkhole. I was chasing a boar and the ground sort of gave way.'

'Are you hurt?'

'No…'

He didn't sound convincing.

'Talen?'

'I can't move my arm, but I'll be fine.'

'Is it broken?'

'I don't know. I don't think so, but it means I can't climb out. There are tunnels down here, but I've no idea where they lead.'

'Stay where you are. We'll come and get you out.'

'How? It's a long way down.'

It was a good question. She looked at Mekki and the Martian shrugged.

'We could rig up a ladder. We have a few cables left over from the escape pod.'

'Ah, no we haven't,' Talen said over the vox-line. 'I used them to make a net... which I... um... lost.'

'Do we have anything else?' Zelia asked.

Mekki shook his head. 'I do not think so.'

Beside them, the servo-sprite was buzzing frantically at Fleapit, as if trying to remind the Jokaero about something. The alien was stubbornly ignoring the flying robot.

'Flegan-Pala?' Mekki asked.

The Jokaero rolled his eyes and reached behind his back. With a click the implants across his spine snapped open, although Fleapit wouldn't let either of them see what he was doing. The metal plates covered a portal to a pocket universe where the Jokaero kept his hidden stash of technology. There was a whoosh and the implants snapped shut again. Fleapit turned his back on them, hiding what was in his hands. He started to work,

Zelia having to wait patiently until he turned and thrust a device towards her.

'Th-thanks... I think,' she said, taking it and turning it over.

'*What is it?*' Talen asked over the vox.

'I honestly don't know,' she was forced to admit. It looked like a pistol, but had a barbed hook pointing out of the barrel, a reel of cable set beneath the grip.

'It is a grappling line,' Mekki informed them before turning to the alien. 'But where did you get the cable, Flegan-Pala?'

The Jokaero didn't answer. Instead, he waddled off to his nest without another word, his long arms wrapped around himself to keep warm.

'What's wrong with him?' Zelia asked.

'He does not like the cold,' Mekki told her.

'*He's not the only one,*' Talen snapped. '*Are you coming to get me out, or what?*'

Snow had started to fall as Mekki and Zelia trudged into the darkening forest, following Talen's signal. The blizzard hadn't struck yet, but it wouldn't be long.

There was no mistaking the hole in the ground when they found it. Zelia approached the edge gingerly, the ground crumbling slightly beneath her feet. Stones loosened and tumbled down, clacking on the bottom of the pit.

'Talen?' she called into the gloom. 'Are you there?'

There was no response.

Cautiously she peered into the chasm, calling his name again. When he still didn't respond, she fished out a lume-rod from beneath her coat and shone it down into the hole.

Talen was nowhere to be seen.

'Do you think he climbed out?'

Mekki activated a lume-bead in the cluster of lenses he wore around his head and swept the light against the cave walls. 'There are plenty of hand-grips, but if he is truly injured...'

'If? You think he's faking?'

'I would not put it past him.'

'Why?'

'To annoy us.'

Zelia shook her head. 'That doesn't seem his style. Yeah, he can be a pain in the backside, but the last thing he ever wants is to show weakness.'

'Then where is he?'

The light from Zelia's lume-rod probed the darkness, settling on a cleft in the cave wall.

'Is that a tunnel?'

Mekki squinted his eyes. 'It is hard to tell.'

'If there's one thing Talen knows, it's tunnels.'

'You think he is trying to find another way out?'

'It's possible.' Passing her lume-rod to Mekki, she thumbed the vox on her sleeve. 'Talen, come in please.'

Her voice echoed up from the pit.

She frowned and tried again. 'Hello?'

The word came back at them again, tinny and with a fraction of a second's delay.

'Say something else,' Mekki instructed her.

'What?'

'Anything. It does not matter.'

Zelia started reciting her favourite nursery rhyme growing up – Five Little Ferro-beasts – and tried to ignore the sound of her words amplified from the belly of the pit.

'There,' Mekki said, pointing the lume-rod in the direction of her echo. Zelia felt a sinking feeling in her stomach when she saw what was lying on the floor.

'Is that... Is that Talen's vox?'

'It would appear so.'

'But why would he leave it behind?'

The Martian's skin was even paler than usual. 'He would not.'

'Something's happened to him,' Zelia said, taking back the lume-rod and stashing it alongside the grappling hook on her bandolier. 'There's no way he'd drop it. Not Talen. He knows how important it is to stay in touch.'

Without another word, she got onto her hands and knees and crawled towards the edge of the precipice. Mekki's eyes widened as he realised what she was considering.

'Zelia Lor, surely you are not thinking of climbing into the cave?'

'Have you got a better idea?' she asked.

'But...'

'I can do this, Mekki. I've been climbing around ruins my entire life.' She indicated to the other side of the chasm. 'You go over there. Shine your lume at the cave wall.'

The Martian opened his mouth to argue, but seemed to realise that she was going anyway. Instead, he circled the hole, positioning himself so he could illuminate Zelia's descent.

She regretted her decision almost immediately. The rock was icy and, despite what Mekki had said, the handholds few and far between. She descended slowly into the darkness, trying not to slip. A couple of times the rock face crumbled, and she had to scramble for a new grip. At one point, she thought she was going to fall, but bit her lip to stop herself from crying out.

'Are you all right?' Mekki shouted down, but she ignored him, concentrating on the climb.

Her arms trembled, and her fingers ached by the time she neared the bottom. She slipped right at the last moment and fell, grunting as she hit the ground. Thankfully it hadn't been far to fall.

'Zelia Lor?' Mekki called down.

'I'm good,' she said, pushing herself up, even though she could already feel the bruises forming. 'Nothing to worry about.'

She pulled out the lume-rod, cursing under her breath when she saw the long cylinder.

'What is it?' Mekki asked from above.

'The rod's cracked,' she told him.
'It must have been when I fell...'
She pressed the toggle and nothing
happened. Well, that was just brilliant.
She shook the cylinder and the light
flickered and activated. It wasn't as
bright as before and kept spluttering on
and off, but it would have to do.

'How are you going to find him?'
Mekki called down.

I've no idea, Zelia thought, but she
wasn't about to admit that. 'I'll stay in
touch.' She crept towards the cleft in
the rock. 'I just wish we'd brought your
servo-sprite.'

'Shall I summon it?' Mekki asked.

'It's a bit too late for that,' she said,
reaching the opening in the wall. She
shone the light in to reveal a narrow
passageway. Yup, definitely a tunnel.
She reached down and picked up
Talen's discarded vox-box and slipped it
into her belt. The thought of venturing

into the passage made her mouth go dry, but if Talen was in trouble she had to help him.

'Good luck,' Mekki called as she disappeared into the tunnel.

I'll need it, Zelia thought. *Talen, where are you?*

CHAPTER THREE

The Den

Talen groaned as he peeled open his eyes. The world was dark around him. He tried to lift his head, but cried out as pain shot down his arm. He grasped his aching shoulder and sat up. Sharp edges cut into his legs. What was he sitting on? A bed of flint? He was obviously still underground. The air was damp, the temperature bitter.

How had he got here? His head felt as if it were full of manufactorum fumes. He'd been in the pit, talking to Zelia on the vox. He put his hand to his belt. The vox-box. It was gone.

It all came flooding back at once.

Zelia telling him to stay where he was, Talen laughing sarcastically. She had called off, leaving Talen alone in the gloom. That's when he had heard it. A growl, rumbling from a tunnel entrance. It was low at first, so faint that Talen thought he had imagined it. Then it had come again, louder and more insistent. This time it had been accompanied by the sound of charging feet. Heavy feet. *Big* feet.

Talen hadn't waited around to find out what it was. Busted arm or not, he'd run to the wall, trying to climb up. It was no good. He couldn't get leverage, not with only one good arm.

Behind him, something had burst from the tunnel, something big. He'd turned to see a monster thundering towards him on powerful arms. He could only remember glimpses of the thing. Broad shoulders. Some kind of carapace on its back. Massive serrated mandibles.

It had brought down a club of a hand, and Talen had blacked out and woken up here.

But where *was* here?

He moved again, wincing as a sharp rock jabbed into his thigh. He grabbed it, frowning as soon as his fingers wrapped around the stone. It didn't feel like slate. He turned it over in his hand, feeling the jagged edge that had tried to pierce his leg, running his fingers along its pitted length until they reached...

Talen threw the shard away, backing up against the wall. That hadn't been a stone. Stones didn't have joints at the end. He groped around the floor, finding what a second ago he might have thought was a large, round rock. He felt the gap where a nose should be, two large sockets, the ridges of pronounced cheekbones. He chucked the thing away, feeling sick as it clacked against the floor. That had been a *skull*. He was surrounded by bones.

Ignoring the pain in his shoulder, Talen scrambled up, trying to ignore the crunch beneath his boots. He kicked something that rustled. Bending down, he explored with his fingers. Was that straw?

He was in the creature's den... or was it a larder?

That's when he heard it. Another growl, not as deep as before. He froze, listening intently. No, it wasn't a growl. It was a snore. Was the monster sleeping nearby? What if it woke up hungry?

He wasn't about to find out. Back on his feet, he walked away from the guttural wheezing, holding his good arm in front of him. There had to be a way out. A gnawed bone crunched beneath his foot and he slipped, crashing back to the floor. He couldn't help but cry out as a fresh bout of pain exploded from his shoulder. He shoved his fist into his mouth, stifling the scream. Whatever was slumbering nearby grunted and turned in its sleep.

It hadn't woken. Not yet. He had to keep quiet.

'Talen? Talen, is that you?'

He didn't know whether to laugh or cry.

'Talen, it's me. Zelia.'

'Shhh,' he hissed. 'Keep your voice down.'

'What?'

He got himself up and stumbled in the direction of her voice. There was a light ahead, bobbing in the darkness. At last he could make out the mouth of the cave. He realised he could also probably turn round and see the dozing monstrosity that had brought him here. It was better he didn't look.

'Talen?'

He hurried forwards, meeting Zelia, who was coming the other way.

'There you are. What happened? We came looking–'

He thrust a filthy hand over her mouth, and her eyes raged with sudden anger. She batted it away, the light from her lume-rod seeming to flash everywhere at once.

'What are you *doing*?'

'Keep it down,' he hissed. 'And stop waving that thing around.' He grabbed her arm and kept it still. 'You'll wake it.'

'Wake what?'

Finally he turned and saw the creature curled up in the middle of a bed of straw and bones. It was smaller than he remembered. Much smaller; barely larger than the boar that had chased him earlier. That didn't make sense.

Unless...

'We need to get out of here,' he told Zelia, attempting to push her back the way she had come. 'Right now.'

But she wouldn't budge. 'Is that an Ambull?' she said, staring at the sleeping creature.

'I don't know, and I don't want to find out. I just want to get out of here.'

'It looks like an infant. Fully grown Ambulls are huge.'

'You don't say. Let's go.'

Zelia shone the torch right at the thing. 'It's hurt.'

'It's *what?*'

She peered at the creature. 'Look at it. It has wounds across its arms and chest. Are those claw marks?'

She was right, but Talen struggled to feel empathy for the alien, especially when it opened its dark eyes and stared straight into the glare from Zelia's torch.

The infant shrieked, which immediately brought a response from deeper in the cave system – the same deep growl Talen had heard in the pit, a growl that immediately turned into a roar.

'Move!' he snapped, and this time Zelia didn't argue. They turned and fled into the tunnel that reverberated with the bellow of a rapidly advancing nightmare.

'Which way back?' Talen asked.

'I don't know,' Zelia responded, looking around wildly. They'd come out in a small cavern that offered a handful of different exits. 'I don't think I came this way.'

The Ambull was gaining on them by the second.

Talen tried not to panic, and closed his eyes, concentrating on his sweating, waxy skin. Yes, there was a breeze, coming from the left.

'This way,' he said, leading the way. They plunged into another tunnel, a glow steadily growing ahead. He followed the light, Zelia at his heels and, seconds later, burst out into the pit.

'There you are,' Mekki said from above them, his pale face appearing over the edge of the hole Talen had created. 'I was beginning to get worried.'

'*You're* worried!' Talen snorted, as another roar came from behind them.

'What is that?' the Martian asked.

'We'll tell you when it's not trying to eat us!' Talen turned to Zelia. 'Well? How are we going to get out?'

'Hold this,' she said, passing him the lume-rod. Once it was in his hand, she pulled out the grapple-gun. Its launcher was made out of what looked like an old bolt rifle.

'Where did Fleapit get *that*?' Talen asked.

'Who knows?' she asked, checking its mechanism.

'Do you at least know how to use it?'

'I may not like guns, but I get the general idea, thanks.'

Raising the launcher, she aimed the grapple's hooks at the umbrella-like caps of the mushroom-trees, high above the hole.

'Will the cable reach all the way up there?' Talen asked.

'There's only one way to find out.'

She pulled the trigger and the hook shot straight up. As the cable unspooled, it flew out of the hole and up into the canopy, embedding itself in one of the caps with a distant *thunk*.

Zelia tested the cable. It seemed strong enough, but would the hook take their weight?

'Now what?' Talen asked.

'You're going to have to hold on to me.'

'You're kidding.'

'Don't worry, I won't bite.'

Another roar reached them, closer than ever.

'Unlike that thing.'

Talen reluctantly grabbed hold of her, putting his good arm around her waist. 'This is so humiliating.'

'Trust me, I'd much rather there was a different way. Mekki, any idea what we do next?'

'There is a button at the back of the grappler,' the Martian shouted down at them. 'Release that and the cable should reel you up.'

'*Should?*' Talen echoed. 'That's reassuring.'

'Are you ready?' Zelia asked.

He nodded and, holding the winch with both hands, she hit the button. With a whine, the cable started to wind in, pulling them up from the ground. At least, that was the idea. All of a sudden, it just stopped, leaving them hanging like bait from a line a few metres from the floor.

'What's happened?' Talen asked.

'It must have got stuck.'

'Can you unstick it?'

She thumbed the release again. 'What do you think I'm trying to do?'

With one final roar, the Ambull burst into the cave, mandibles clicking furiously. It was bigger than Talen remembered, its claws longer and sharper, and it was coming straight for them!

CHAPTER FOUR

In the Nick of Time

Zelia pressed hard on the cable release.
With a click, the cable whirred into life
again and they rocketed up, narrowly
missing a swipe from the monster's
long talons.

The creature bayed in fury as they
shot out of the hole, Zelia stopping the
winch so they swung like a pendulum
over the pit.

'Grab us,' Zelia yelled at Mekki, who
lunged for them, but missed. They
swung back over the hole, trying to
gather enough momentum to swing
back towards Mekki. Zelia's arms ached,
but that was nothing compared to the

pain Talen must have been enduring.

They swayed back towards Mekki, but the cable snapped, finally giving out. They tumbled forwards, landing in the snow rather than falling back down to the waiting monster.

'Let's never do that again,' Talen breathed, swatting Mekki's hands out of the way as the Martian tried to help him up.

'Deal,' Zelia agreed, glancing down at the horror in the cave. Far below them, the Ambull threw back its head and howled at the light. From up here, they could see it was missing a claw, blood crusted around deep gashes across its chest. Furious that its prey had escaped, it threw itself at the cave wall and tried to clamber up, only to tumble back down again.

Still it didn't give up, its remaining claws slicing deep into the rock.

'You don't think it can get up here, do you?' Talen asked.

'No,' Mekki said. 'But I suggest we get

back... just in case.'

The blizzard was starting to rage by the time they arrived at the camp. They could barely see as they struggled past the sonic posts, the servo-sprite reactivating the sound-wall from the shelter of the dome.

Spluttering with the cold, they bundled inside, Mekki closing the hatch behind them. The glow-orbs Fleapit had installed in the walls flickered, the heater at the centre of the room struggling to warm the space. The servo-sprite did its best to boost the filaments but it was obvious that the powercells were nearly exhausted.

'So, what *was* that thing?' Talen said, gasping as he sat on one of the bunks that Fleapit had fashioned from the escape pod's benches.

Zelia shrugged off her thermo-coat. 'The Ambull? They're aliens found on desert worlds. They live underground, burrowing through the rock with their claws.' She pulled the omniscope from her bandolier. 'Mum warned me about them on an expedition to Huttama, but we never encountered any, thank the Emperor.'

Talen nodded at the walls of the dome, which shuddered against the storm. 'This isn't a desert.'

'No, but there's loads we don't know about aliens. It must have adapted itself for cold weather. Whatever it was doing here, did you see the claw marks across its chest?'

'Just like its kid.'

'Something attacked them down there.'

'Who would take on something that big?' He winced, as more pain lanced across his shoulders.

'Talen?'

'It's nothing.'

Zelia walked over to him. 'Take off your coat.'

'Why?'

'I need to examine your shoulder.'

'When did you become a doctor?'

She indicated the device in her hand. 'This does more than just magnify. Keep it folded up and it doubles as a medi-scanner.'

'Handy.'

'Never had to use it until now.' She turned to Mekki. 'Can you help Talen take off his vest?'

'I can manage,' Talen insisted, struggling – and failing – to remove his armless jacket. 'Actually, no... I can't.'

Carefully, Mekki eased the patch-covered jacket over Talen's swollen shoulder.

'Let's see what you've done,' said Zelia, leaning over Talen. Putting the lens right up to his shoulder, she peered through the viewfinder.

'Well?' he asked.

She stood back up, twisting the scope's case. The lens glowed, projecting a hololithic image of the bones in Talen's shoulder in front of them, like a three-dimensional X-ray.

'Wow,' Talen said, genuinely impressed.

'At least we can see that it's not broken,' Zelia said.

'No, but I'm guessing it's not supposed to look like that.'

The ball of Talen's upper arm bone had popped completely out of its socket.

'*Diagnosis,*' the scope's internal cogitator said, in a perfect rendition of Elise Lor's voice. '*Complete dislocation. The joint must be replaced as soon as possible.*'

'Replaced?' Talen said, not liking the sound of that at all.

'Put back into its socket,' Zelia explained.

'Is it difficult?' Talen asked.

'We could ask Flegan-Pala?' Mekki suggested.

'No!' Talen replied, a little too quickly. 'I still don't trust him. Not really.'

'You're kidding,' Zelia said. 'After everything he's done for us?'

He looked at her. 'Can't you do it?'

'Me?'

He glanced at the omniscope. 'There must be something in that box of tricks that tells you what to do.'

The thought of it made her feel sick.

'Actually, I believe I can be of assistance,' Mekki said. 'In case of emergencies, the escape pod's machine-spirit has a full medical database.'

Talen frowned. 'Machine-spirit?'

'He means the cogitator,' Zelia told him. 'Tech-speak.'

Mekki walked over to the shelter's main terminal and connected the haptic implants on the end of his fingers to the access ports. The electoos on his head and arm shone as he communed with the cogitator, images flashing onto the terminal's display.

'I have successfully located the treatment for a dislocated shoulder,' he announced after a few moments.

Zelia read the instructions, feeling more than a little queasy. Not for the first time, she wished that her mum was there.

Behind her, Talen had stood up nervously. 'So, what do we have to do?'

Zelia's mouth was dry, but she knew she had no choice. 'I'm not going to lie to you,' she said, turning to face him. 'This is probably going to hurt.'

'Can't be any worse than it feels now.'

She wasn't sure about that. 'Are you ready?'

'No... but let's do it before I change my mind.'

CHAPTER FIVE

Plunged Into Darkness

Talen Stormweaver could be annoying, but no one could say he wasn't brave. He lay on the floor, barely whimpering as Zelia followed the cogitator's instructions. He only cried out when she clicked his shoulder back into place.

Mekki packed snow into a blanket, pressing it against his bruised shoulder to numb the pain, and Zelia pretended she didn't see the tears in his eyes.

When the snow had melted, Mekki dried the blanket and used the fabric to make a sling. It was moments like this that gave Zelia a swell of hope. When she thought about what they had overcome so far – shipwreck, attack and now injury – she was sure they'd survive long enough to be rescued. They'd become quite a team, despite all the quarrelling. For all they knew, her mum was out there somewhere, searching the stars for them in the *Scriptor*. Maybe she'd already locked on to the beacon's signal.

They sat in silence for a while, the only sound the whirr of the servo-sprite's wings and the wind that raged outside. Zelia made Talen eat some of the rations, even though the ganger insisted he wasn't hungry. He needed to keep his strength up if his shoulder was going to recover.

Zelia was curled up on her bunk, almost drifting off to sleep, when the glow-orbs suddenly went out.

'What's happened?' she called out.

'It is the powercells,' Mekki replied, his face illuminated by the green light of his wrist-screen.

'Are they dead?' Zelia asked.

Mekki didn't reply. Instead, he flicked on the illuminated frame of one of the lenses he wore on his head and rushed over to the main terminal. He slipped the haptic implants into the access points and within seconds the glow-orbs flickered back on, although the light was greasy and the orbs noticeably not as bright.

'Well done, Mekki,' Zelia said, sighing in relief. 'I didn't like the idea of being in the dark – not in the middle of this storm.'

Mekki pulled his fingers from the terminal. 'We might be soon. The cells are almost drained.'

'Can we cut back on anything so they last longer?'

The Martian looked doubtful. 'We are down to the bare minimum already. We currently have light, heating and protection through the sonic fence. Plus, the beacon needs power to operate.'

'The beacon that no one's answering,' Talen pointed out.

Mekki continued without hesitation. 'Even if we shut down two or three essential systems, the powercells will be exhausted in a day.'

Talen ran his fingers through his hair. 'Isn't there anything you can do? I thought you were at one with the machine-spirits?'

Mekki's mouth became a thin line at Talen's mocking tone. 'I have done as much as I can. I am not a miracle worker.'

'No,' Zelia said. 'But I know who is. If you can't think of a way to preserve power, maybe Fleapit can.'

Getting to Fleapit's nest was easier said than done. The storm had plunged the mountainside into a whiteout. Wrapped in their coats, the children stumbled into the blizzard, but could barely see each other, let alone Fleapit's tent. Within minutes they were lost in their own camp.

'Can't you contact him?' Talen yelled,

trying to be heard over the gale.

'What?' Mekki called back.

'You know,' Talen replied, tapping his head. 'Use your techie-mumbo-jumbo.'

If Mekki heard, he didn't respond.

'Over here,' Zelia shouted, somewhere ahead of Talen. 'I've found the nest.'

'Where are you?'

'Follow my voice.'

Yeah, 'cause don't you love using it, Talen thought to himself as he pushed against the wind. Zelia meant well, he knew she did. And she'd sorted out his arm, more or less – but she was just so bossy. All his life he'd been told what to do. First his dad, then Onak, and now her! And to think, he'd run away from home to be free. Some chance. The universe was obviously trying to tell him something.

Talen cried out in pain as he stumbled into Mekki. 'Watch it!'

'Watch what? You are as blind as I am, Talen Stormweaver.'

'Just Talen, okay? Why do you always

have to speak like that?'

'What is wrong with you two?' Zelia shouted, appearing out of the snow to separate them. 'Haven't we got enough to deal with? Come on.' She started to walk back in the direction she'd come, pausing when she realised the two boys were still locked in a staring competition. 'Come. On.'

'All right, all right,' Talen said, finally trudging towards her. He didn't know if Mekki was following, and cared even less.

Zelia was holding Fleapit's tent open. Talen ducked inside. The canvas walls were thick and well insulated. Where had the alien found those? And what else did he have stashed in that inter-dimensional backpack of his?

It was a tight squeeze. The poles supporting the tent strained against the wind, pressing the already-low ceiling down on them. Zelia clicked on her lume-rod, the yellow light revealing Fleapit curled up on a bed of cables and wires. Tools were dotted everywhere – power-hammers, vibro-drivers and other devices – and the entire place reeked of animal.

'Fleapit?' she said quietly, like a mother trying to wake a sleeping baby. 'Fleapit, wake up.'

The Jokaero didn't stir.

'Oi,' Talen said, kicking the nest of cables.

'Talen!' she hissed.

'What?' he replied, trying to look innocent. 'You were the one who wanted to wake him up.'

The Jokaero slumbered on, the canvas flapping noisily in the wind.

'How can he sleep through this racket anyway?'

Mekki crouched down beside the snoozing Jokaero. 'I do not think Flegan-Pala is asleep.'

Zelia dropped down beside the Martian. 'Oh no. You don't mean he's–'

'No.' Mekki raised a hand to cut off her question. 'He is not dead, but he is not alive either.'

'What does that mean?' Talen asked.

Mekki reached over and gently stroked the Jokaero's fur with his haptic implants. 'He has put himself into a form of suspended animation. For all intents and purposes, Flegan-Pala is hibernating.'

'Why?' Zelia asked.

'To escape the cold?' Mekki suggested. 'Flegan-Pala's joints have been troubling him over the last few days. He has had difficulty walking.'

'I haven't noticed,' Talen admitted.

'Maybe you should be more observant,' Mekki sniffed.

'*Please* don't start again,' Zelia begged them.

'My apologies,' Mekki said, to Zelia rather than Talen, before turning his attention back to the Jokaero. 'According to the servo-sprite, his implants are also causing him trouble. We know so little about how Flegan-Pala operates. Perhaps the low temperatures are interfering with his... systems.'

'I know how he feels,' Talen muttered. 'They're interfering with mine too.'

Zelia stood up beside him. 'Talen, please...'

'What? Am I supposed to feel sorry for the ape?'

'Not an ape,' Mekki corrected.

'Does it matter?' Talen shouted back.

'Yes!' Zelia said before Mekki could respond. 'Yes, it does. Fleapit's not an animal. He's part of our team.'

Talen laughed. 'We're a *team* now?'

'Of course we are. And don't forget

where we'd be *without* Fleapit. The shelter. The beacons. That's all him.'

'With a little help,' Mekki pointed out quietly.

'Well, he wasn't thinking of the team when he decided to have a nap, was he?' Talen argued, talking over the Martian. 'If he's the one keeping us alive, then what's going to happen now? Who's going to keep the power going?'

'I can do it,' Mekki insisted.

'You?' Talen scoffed. 'You said it yourself, you're out of your depth. You need the fuzzball as much as we do. What happens when the powercells finally give up, or we run out of food?'

Now Mekki was on his feet, his grey eyes flashing with anger. 'At least I did not waste rations on a fool's errand!'

'A what?' Talen jabbed a finger at the Martian. 'Do you mean the hunt? I was trying to find us proper food!'

'But, instead we had to rescue you from a hole in the ground. We should have left you where you were.'

'Fine,' Zelia said, raising her hands in surrender. 'You want to fight, then fight. I don't care any more. If Fleapit really is out of action, then we're going to need to work together, now more than ever. But if you can't handle that...'

'You know, maybe I can't,' Talen said, pulling open the tent. He needed to get out of here before he really did hit someone. 'You two do what you want. It's all just a waste of time anyway.'

Talen didn't sleep well that night. None of them did. The heater had packed up almost as soon as they'd tried to settle down. They lay huddled on their bunks using the thermo-coats as blankets, their backs to each other.

Zelia had sat talking to her omniscope for a while, pretending she was trying to find out more about Fleapit's species. Talen knew what she was really doing. She wanted to hear her mum's voice, even if it was only a voice print.

'Give it a rest, will you?' he snapped

at her. 'I'm trying to sleep.'

He'd pretended not to hear her crying in the darkness. He wanted to go over to her, to say he was sorry, but didn't have the words. At least she couldn't see him clutching the toy Guardsman his brother had given him all those years ago, or the tears that pricked his own eyes.

Had he really meant what he'd said to them? Were they really wasting their time?

They'd get off this planet, one way or another... wouldn't they?

CHAPTER SIX

01001110

'No! Get away from me!'

Zelia sat up, bashing her head on the ledge above her bunk.

'Zelia Lor?'

Rubbing her scalp, she looked up to see Mekki hunched over the heater. Talen was on his bunk, his coat wrapped around him and his back still towards her.

'I-I'm all right. It was just a dream.'

Satisfied with the answer, Mekki went back to work.

Just a dream? Who was she trying to kid? It was more like a *nightmare*, the same nightmare that had plagued her every night since Erasmus died. She hadn't witnessed his sacrifice first hand, but that didn't stop her overactive imagination filling in the details. Erasmus and the Hunter facing a tsunami of rushing snow. The Hunter turning to leap for the older man, its single eye flaring as the avalanche hit. Cold talons biting into Erasmus's arms, a rictus grin on the Necron's face.

'*You think you've won, fleshling. Think you're so clever.*'

And then the Necron was in the dome, freed from its icy tomb. Looming over her bed. Frozen steel burning her skin as it grabbed her arms.

'*Give me the Diadem, child. Give me the—*'

That's when she had woken, confused and disorientated. Always the same dream.

Zelia rubbed her eyes and stretched, her body aching in the cold. At the centre of the dome, Mekki pushed over the heater in frustration.

'Mekki?' Zelia pushed off her coat and moved to him. She knew better than to place a comforting hand on his shoulder. The Martian didn't like to be touched. 'What's wrong?'

The pale-skinned boy glared down at the powerless heater. 'I have been trying to fix this.'

'How are you getting on?'

Now his glare flicked up to her. 'How do you think?'

She raised her hands as if in surrender. 'Mekki, you're doing your best.'

'Then my best is not good enough.' He stood up, his entire body rigid. She had never seen him like this. Mekki was usually so calm, so controlled. 'None of Flegan-Pala's constructs make sense to me. They are like nothing I have seen before.'

She got to her feet beside him. 'That's hardly surprising. He's... well, he's not like us. Who knows how all this works?'

Mekki slapped his narrow chest.

'I should know. I have worked with machines all my life. But all this...' He looked around the darkened dome, his eyes glistening. 'This is nonsense.'

'You're being too hard on yourself.'

'Am I?' He got up and walked over to the hatch. 'Look at these,' he said, pointing towards the web of cables that were tacked over the shelter's curved walls. 'What is their purpose?'

She shrugged. 'I don't know.'

'Neither do I. And I should. Flegan-Pala's techniques are... They are a mystery to me.'

Opening an access panel, he thrust his haptic implants into the cogitator ports. 'What do the cables do? What is their function?' His face was twisted into a snarl, his teeth clenched. Sparks fizzed around his fingertips as he pushed his implants deeper. 'Flegan-Pala was building something. What was it? *What was it?*'

Zelia reached forwards to grab him, whether Mekki liked being touched or not. The boy was shaking, muttering a language Zelia had never heard before. Was that... *binaric*? A series of noughts and ones?

'Mekki, you need to stop. You're scaring me. You need to calm down.'

'No,' he shouted, pushing her away. She tumbled back, landing awkwardly on the heater. When she looked up he was looming over her like the Hunter in her dream, his usually placid features contorted with anger. 'You always tell me what to do. You are not your mother, Zelia Lor. You are not my mistress.'

Tears stung her eyes. 'Mekki, I–'

He whirled around, beating his fists against his head. His speech was a mixture of numbers and words, spoken so quickly that Zelia could barely follow them.

'01001110... Need to know... need... 01100001... answers.'

She tried to reach up to him, but he was already opening the hatch. Before

she could stop him, he stumbled into
the storm, disappearing from view. He
didn't even have his thermo-coat.

'Mekki, wait. You'll freeze. *Mekki!*'

The cold wind hit Mekki like a slap
in the face. Even as the hatch closed
behind him, he wondered what he was
doing. He threw his hands around
himself, his scarlet robes instantly
drenched by the snow.

But he could not go back into the
dome. He would not. He needed to fix
things, he needed to put things right.
The way he had talked to Zelia Lor...
The things he had said...

He needed to step up. He needed to
be strong.

Flipping down a pair of protective
lenses over his eyes, Mekki pushed
further into the storm, heading in
what he hoped was the direction of
Flegan-Pala's nest. He could feel the
servos of his exo-frame seizing up as
he blundered on. Within seconds, even

the lenses were covered in frost. He brushed them clear with numb fingers.

The storm stole away his cry as he thudded into something tall. He reached out and touched the post. It was one of Flegan-Pala's sonic generators. He was at the sound-wall, but it was not working. The power had failed.

Something moved within the perimeter. He looked up, and saw a shadow moving in the snow. Was it Zelia? Had she come to find him? He called out, but there was no reply.

The shadow looked tall... too tall for Zelia. And there was something else, something wrong about the way she was standing. At first Mekki could not work out what it was, and then it struck him. Her arms. Why did she have four arms?

He gasped and took a step back. That wasn't Zelia. Something was out here in the snow with him. Something that wasn't human.

'Zelia Lor!' he shouted. 'Talen

Stormweaver! Somebody, help me!'

This could not be happening. He started to babble, a relentless stream of binaric, his comfort in times of stress.

The thing in the snow lurched forwards. Mekki screamed out, and then saw an eye through the blizzard. It was looking straight at him. Suddenly the world seemed to soften. The wind. The cold. The snow. Even the fear. It melted away, as if it did not matter at all. Mekki's breath slowed, as did the numbers in his head. His chapped lips drew back into a smile. It was going to be all right. All the panic was gone. All the anxiety. He barely even noticed the creature's teeth or its claws or the long tongue that flicked forwards.

'Mekki!'

A voice cut through his trance, dragging him back to the storm. He shook his head as if waking from a dream. What was he doing out here?

'Mekki, where are you?'

Zelia was looking for him, but she was not alone.

'Mekki! Where are you, Cog-Boy?'

The ganger was with her. They were out in the storm.

They were in danger.

Mekki ran, nearly knocking Zelia down as he floundered into her.

'Mekki? What are you doing? You're frozen!'

He could barely speak. 'Get... inside,' he stammered, his teeth chattering wildly. His knees were starting to buckle.

The ganger grabbed him, keeping

him on his feet. 'If I catch my death because I had to come out here to find you...' he began.

'Death...' Mekki interrupted. 'In the snow... It is coming!'

Even through the blizzard, Mekki could see Zelia frown beneath her hood. 'What are you talking about?'

'M-monster...'

'You mean Fleapit?' Talen joked. 'Has the walking rug woken up?'

'No... M-monster... in the snow.'

'You're seeing things,' the ganger told him. 'That big brain of yours has frozen solid.'

A roar came from behind them. It was not like the roar of the Ambull. It was not even like the roar of the Necron. It was different, and it was deadly.

'There *is* something out here,' Zelia exclaimed, grabbing his arm. 'Talen, help me get him inside.'

'But where is inside?' the ganger replied.

'Over there! Run!'

CHAPTER SEVEN

The Genestealer

Running in a snowdrift had been bad enough. Running in a blizzard was worse. At least in the mushroom forest Talen could see where he was going, and what was chasing him.

'Is it the Ambull?' he asked as they floundered back to the dome.

'Don't think so,' Zelia replied. 'They don't normally venture up to the surface.'

'Since when is anything on this planet normal?'

'Good point.'

A light blazed in front of them. The hatch!

'Go,' he shouted, pushing Mekki and Zelia over the threshold. He glanced back and saw a shadow looming towards them. He leapt after them, crying out with pain as he pulled the hatch shut.

'Talen, your shoulder...' Zelia said.

'I'm fine,' he gasped, waving away her concern. 'So, if that's not an Ambull out there, what is it?'

Whatever it was threw itself at the hatch. Claws raked against metal, guttural snarls barely muffled by the thick door.

'Still think Mekki's seeing things?' Zelia gasped.

The Martian was standing staring at the door and shaking from head to foot. Talen grabbed Mekki's coat and threw it over him.

'What was it?'

'It had four arms,' Mekki stammered. 'With l-long claws.'

'Thanks...' Talen grunted. 'That's helpful.'

'Actually, it might be,' Zelia said, turning to the half-frozen Martian. 'Mekki, do you remember the dig on Krelos, the temple ship that mum and Erasmus were excavating?'

Mekki nodded, although it was hard to tell as the Martian was shaking so much.

'Do you still have a copy of the catalogue?'

'The what?' Talen asked.

'Mekki records everything we find, remember?' Zelia replied.

The Martian shrugged off his coat. 'In my pack. Next to the magna-extractor...'

Zelia moved around the back of him and opened his backpack to search. 'In the leather wallet?'

He nodded. 'Yes.'

She pulled out a battered leather folder and handed it to Mekki. He opened it carefully on his bunk, revealing dozens of data-cards.

'What are they?' Talen asked.

'Memory wafers,' Mekki told him,

choosing one and slotting it into his wrist-screen. 'Accessing,' he said, his frost-encrusted electoos glowing as he tapped the display.

'Look for the skeleton we found near the flight deck,' Zelia said.

The monster kept throwing itself against the wall.

'We don't have time for this,' Talen said, staring at the wall-panels. The mesh of wires jangled with every blow.

Mekki's holo-projector flicked down from his collection of lenses and a hololith appeared in front of them. The electronic image flickered before solidifying into a pile of rusty crates.

'What good is that?' Talen asked as the hatch continued to shudder.

Mekki swiped across the screen with a finger. The hololith switched to the image of a rusty helm half buried in sand, and then fragments of broken pipe, followed by a mechanical grabber.

'No,' the Martian said, as he scrolled through the three-dimensional images.

'No. No. No... Yes!'

A hololithic skeleton appeared on the floor. The bones were scattered, but they clearly formed a figure... a figure with four arms.

'That's it,' Zelia said. 'That's the alien.'

Her mum's voice crackled out of the wrist-screen.

'Subject displays a bulbous skull, with a curved spinal column and two sets of arms. The first is equipped with almost human hands while the other features incredibly strong claws.'

'Can we hurry this up?' Talen urged.

'What did mum call it?' Zelia asked Mekki. 'A gene... gene...'

'Genestealer,' Mekki remembered.

'That's it!' Zelia clapped her hands together. 'A Genestealer.'

'And what's a Genestealer?' Talen asked.

'No idea,' Zelia admitted. 'But it's obviously alien.'

'I could have told you that before the light-show.'

Above them, the servo-sprite squealed as the Genestealer's purple claws sliced clean through the wall.

'Mum wasn't joking about how strong they were,' Zelia said as the alien hacked at the hole it had created.

'This is stupid,' Talen said, looking around for a weapon. 'I'm not standing here while that thing carves a new door!' He ran to his bunk, standing the bench on its end.

'What are you going to do with that?' Zelia asked.

Talen wasn't quite sure. 'I don't know. Try to block the hole, maybe? Use it as a shield?'

'A shield!' Mekki repeated, his eyes wide with realisation.

'Yeah. Unless you've a better idea.'

'No. You do not understand,' Mekki said, rushing for the access panel near the hatch. 'That is what Flegan-Pala was constructing before he went into hibernation.' He indicated the wires on the walls. 'It is a shield... a *force field.*'

'Like the sonic fence?' Zelia asked, not taking her eyes off the flashing claws.

'No.' Mekki was racing around the shelter, checking one cluster of wires after another, all signs that he nearly froze to death gone. 'The sonic fence creates noise to frighten away predators, but a force field is made of pure energy. I have never seen one before.'

'Which is why you didn't know what Fleapit was doing!'

The Martian and his sprite were working as one, completing the circuits on the walls. 'Flegan-Pala's techniques are still a mystery,' Mekki admitted. 'This will either work... or the shelter will explode.'

'That's comforting,' Talen said, hiding behind the upturned bench. The Genestealer had thrust a long arm through the ragged hole and was grasping for them across the shelter. Talen caught glimpses of a monstrous face as it tried to break in. Its leathery

skin was the purple of a bruise, a ridge
of even darker scales running down
a domed forehead. A fresh scar ran
through one of its pupilless eyes and
a long, pointed tongue flicked out past
bared teeth, each as sharp as a needle.

Beside him, Zelia looked around
frantically, her eyes falling on piping
that ran up the centre of the dome.

'Is this part of Fleapit's circuit?' she
asked Mekki.

The Martian glanced up at the pipe. 'I
do not think so.'

'Good. Talen, help me.'

'With what?' the ganger asked.

Zelia tugged at the curved pipe, trying to yank it from the wall. 'I thought you were the one who liked weapons.'

Talen grinned. 'Now you're talking.'

He ran across and helped pull at the pipe with her. The clips holding it to the wall twisted before releasing the metal tubing with a sharp snap. Zelia separated the pipe into shorter segments, and passed one to him.

'Not exactly a spud-jacker,' she said.

He took the pipe and slapped it against his palm. 'But heavy enough.'

'For what?' Mekki asked.

'To buy you time,' Zelia said, running towards the Genestealer's grasping hand. She brought her pipe down on the alien's wrist, the impact producing a satisfying crunch. Talen joined in, avoiding the slashing claws. The xenos hissed and snarled, its hand whipping around to swipe Zelia's pipe from her grip. Talen batted its claws away before they could slice into her.

'Mekki,' he urged, dodging back as he was nearly disembowelled. 'You need to hurry up.'

Mekki looked up at the servo-sprite, which appeared to nod at him.

'Well?' Zelia asked, snatching her length of pipe from the floor. 'Are you done?'

'It would appear so.'

'Will it blow up?' Talen asked, thwacking the alien's hand.

'Impossible to tell,' the Martian admitted.

'Then just do it,' Zelia said.

Mekki thrust his haptic implants into the last jumble of cables. There was a crackle of static and Talen felt the hairs on his arms stand on end. It was as if the air itself was being electrified.

With a flash of light the scar-faced monster was thrown violently back. Something slapped to the floor. The Genestealer's arm had been sliced off by Mekki's force field. It twitched

horribly for a moment and then lay
still.

With a pained roar, the Genestealer
raked the dome with its remaining
claws. There was another, even brighter
flash and the monster was knocked
back again.

'You did it,' Zelia cheered, pulling
Mekki into a hug whether he wanted
one or not. 'You made a force field.'

'No,' Mekki insisted, although there
was no disguising the satisfied look on
his pale face. 'Flegan-Pala made a force
field. I simply completed it.'

'I don't care who did what,' Talen
said, gingerly poking the severed limb
with his pipe, 'as long as it holds.'

Mekki nodded. 'It will, as long as the
powercells function.'

Talen didn't like the sound of that.
'You mean the same powercells that
were almost empty, the ones we needed
Fleapit to fix?'

Mekki busied himself with his screen.
'Yes.'

'And how long do we have?' Zelia asked.

The Martian cocked his head as he made his calculations. 'Approximately forty minutes.'

'Forty minutes?' Talen spluttered. 'And then Scarface will be able to claw himself in? You know, the alien we've just made *really* angry?'

'Correct.'

Talen felt sick. 'So, we're trapped.'

Outside, the Genestealer was pacing back and forth in the snow, its back hunched as it clutched the stump where its arm had been. As Talen watched, it stopped, and stared right at him.

Their eyes met through the hole in the wall, and suddenly things didn't seem so bad. Talen's arm dropped to his side, the section of pipe slipping from his fingers. He barely heard it clatter against the floor.

What was he worrying about? So, the Genestealer was waiting for them, out there in the blizzard? Did that matter?

Did anything matter?

Images flashed through Talen's mind. Targian exploding. The Hunter stalking through the forest. Fleapit pulling the Necron Diadem from Erasmus's satchel.

None of that was important. None of the danger or the arguments. Voices raised, shouting.

You're out of your depth.

At least I did not waste rations on a fool's errand.

The same argument, going around and around in his head.

The Genestealer would make that all go away, all the fear and regret. The Genestealer wasn't evil. It was his friend.

All Talen had to do was go outside.

CHAPTER EIGHT

Under the Thrall

Zelia watched in horror as Talen shuffled towards the hole in the wall. His face was slack, his limbs loose, as if he were sleepwalking.

'Talen? Talen, what are you doing?'

She tried to grab him, but he shrugged her off, lumbering towards the Genestealer that was waiting patiently in the snow.

'What's wrong with him?'

'It is the alien,' Mekki told her. 'When I was outside, I looked into its eyes and lost myself.'

'What do you mean?'

'I felt only calm, no fear at all.'

'It hypnotises its victims so they can't escape,' Zelia realised. 'We have to break its hold over him.'

She stood in front of Talen, waving her hands in front of the boy's face. 'Hey, Talen, look at me. It's Ladle-Girl. Remember me?'

Talen just shoved her out of the way and kept shuffling forwards.

'All right, so that didn't work...' She looked around and saw Talen's bed, still standing on its end like a shield. Suddenly she knew what to do. 'Mekki, help me.'

Rushing to the bunk, she scooped up Talen's discarded coat and threw it across the metal bed. Then she and Mekki pushed the upturned bench across the floor, pressing it against the hole, blocking the view of the Genestealer.

The effect was instantaneous. Talen stopped, unsteady on his feet.

'W-what... what's happening?'

'You were in a trance,' Zelia told him.

'The Genestealer got inside your head. You were going outside.'

'No...' He shook his head. 'That's... impossible. I wouldn't do that.'

She placed a hand on his good arm. 'It's all right, Talen. It happened to Mekki too, out in the snow.'

'Although I managed to shake it off by myself,' the Martian added, unhelpfully.

Zelia glared at him. 'You were blinded by the storm. Perhaps the Genestealer needs to see its victims clearly for the trance to work.' She turned back to the dazed ganger. 'What did you call it, Talen? Can you remember?'

Talen blinked, as if trying to clear his vision. 'Um... Scarface?'

'Yes,' she said, seizing on the name. 'Scarface. Do you remember? Do you remember who we are?'

'Yeah,' he said, rubbing his eyes. 'You're a pain in the backside.'

'He has recovered,' Mekki stated flatly.

Behind Zelia's temporary barrier, Scarface bayed in frustration. There was a burst of energy, followed by another and another. The entire dome shook, but the force field held, even as the Genestealer threw itself repeatedly at the shelter. The three children huddled together at the centre of the dome as the onslaught continued. The wires on the walls sparked and fizzed, the servo-sprite flitting around to check the force field was still functioning.

'Why won't it stop?' Zelia said, as the attacks became more and more frenzied.

Mekki checked his wrist-screen. 'It is trying to drain the power.'

'Until there's nothing left,' said Talen.

The glow-orbs flickered, the walls quaking and sparks raining down. Zelia was shocked to feel Talen's hand slip into hers. They stood shoulder to shoulder, their fingers laced together, until the attacks just stopped.

The children stood in silence, eyes

wide, ears straining to hear.

'What happened to it?' Zelia finally whispered.

Mekki turned to the servo-sprite. 'Check outside.'

The tiny robot flew over to the upturned bed and squeezed through a gap between the coat and the wall. None of them even dared to breathe as they listened to the sprite buzzing outside.

Talen looked at Mekki. 'Well?'

The Martian boy's eyes misted over, his electoos flashing. 'The alien is not outside...' He paused, silently communicating with the sprite before concluding: 'It is gone.'

'To lick its wounds?' Zelia asked.

'Most probably.'

Talen pulled his hand free. 'But what if it comes back?'

Mekki checked his screen. 'The powercells *are* almost exhausted.'

'And we have no way to, you know, recharge them?'

'Not without specialist equipment.'

'And that's what I don't understand,' Zelia said. 'Where did Fleapit get the components to build the force field in the first place, not to mention all those cables in his nest?'

'And this as well,' Mekki said, kneeling by the overturned heater. 'It contains components that do not belong to the escape pod.' He prised open the machine's casing and pulled out a metal coil. 'See? There is an engraving on this unit.'

He passed Zelia the mechanism, pointing out tiny writing on the side.

'Is it alien?' Talen asked. 'Could it be from the Necron's ship? It must have had one, right?'

Zelia shook her head. 'It doesn't match the markings on the Hunter's chest, or the fighters we saw on Targian.' She used her omniscope to magnify the letters. 'Registry number one-eight-zero-four,' she said, reading aloud. 'It's human.'

'And you're sure it's not from the *Mercator*?' Talen asked.

'As far as I can tell,' Mekki replied.

'So where did it come from?'

'From the woods,' Zelia said suddenly. 'Fleapit's been wandering into the forest, looking for salvage. What if he found something out there?'

'Why would he keep it secret?' Mekki asked.

'But he hasn't,' Zelia said. 'He's been taking the servo-sprite with him.'

Mekki stood and pressed a button on his wrist-display. Seconds later, the tiny robot buzzed back through the breach in the wall.

'Has Flegan-Pala found another source of technology?' Mekki asked the automaton.

The sprite bobbed nervously in the air.

'Well?' Zelia prompted.

Mekki looked astonished. 'Flegan-Pala has put a block on the sprite's memory. It... cannot answer me.'

'I told you we couldn't trust him,'

Talen said. 'He's been lying to us all this time. Something's out there, in the forest. That's where he keeps going.'

'But how will it help us?' Zelia asked.

Mekki took the coil back from her. 'I would have thought that was obvious. If we can discover his source, we may find something to restore the powercells or improve our defences,' he explained.

'There's only one problem.' Zelia glanced over at the bunk resting against the wall.

Talen swallowed. 'It means going out there... with Scarface still on the prowl.'

She nodded.

Talen sighed. 'I'd feel happier if we had something to fight with.' He looked around, spotting the grapple-launcher next to Zelia's bunk. 'Could we do something with this?' he asked, picking up the launcher. 'Turn it back into a bolter or something?'

Zelia shifted uncomfortably. 'I'm not sure.'

Talen rolled his eyes. 'Because you don't like guns? Grow up, Zelia.'

'Shush,' Mekki hissed.

Talen ignored the Martian, pointing towards the alien arm on the floor. 'Besides, I don't think Scarface is a pacifist. What are you going to do? Ask him nicely to leave us alone?'

'I said shush,' Mekki repeated.

Zelia sighed and took the launcher from Talen. 'No, Talen's right. We need to defend ourselves.'

'We need to be quiet,' the Martian snapped. 'Listen!'

Talen frowned. 'To what?'

Zelia cocked her head. 'He's right. There's a scrabbling noise...'

Talen swallowed, backing away from the dismantled heater. 'Beneath the ground! What is it?'

'I do not know,' admitted Mekki, 'but I think we are about to find out.'

As they watched, a hand burst up

through the floor – a hand with three
sharp claws.

CHAPTER NINE

Caged

With a roar, Scarface pushed itself up from the widening crack in the floor. That's why the Genestealer had gone quiet. It had been digging under the force field, tunnelling through solid rock!

'Everybody out,' Zelia yelled, grabbing her coat.

Talen had already pulled his from the upturned bunk and was struggling to open the hatch.

'Wait,' Mekki snapped, tapping his wrist-screen.

'No way,' Talen replied, looking back at the monster that was clambering from the hole, fragments of rock tumbling from its hunched body. It was almost out.

'You cannot open the hatch while the force field is active,' the Martian told them.

'Then deactivate it,' Zelia demanded.

Mekki tapped out a sequence on his display, the servo-sprite flitting around him. There was a crackle and the force field fell silent.

'There,' he said. 'Go.'

'Finally!' Talen grunted as he pushed

against the heavy door. Scarface leapt from the hole, its foot catching on a rock.

'Hurry,' Zelia said, helping the ganger. The hatch swung open and they fell out the door. Mekki jumped out after them and grabbed the hatch, the servo-sprite on his shoulder.

The Genestealer broke free and raced for the door. Mekki brought the hatch down on its brutal face. It slammed itself against the door, claws trying to prise the hatch open.

'Run!' shouted Talen, but Mekki went back to his screen. He jabbed a control and the force field reactivated.

'What good is that?' Talen asked.

'Watch,' said Mekki calmly.

Snarling, Scarface knocked the upturned bed from the hole in the wall and tried to squeeze through. The force field flared, throwing the Genestealer back from the hole. The alien ran at the breach once more, and again received a shock.

'I have reversed the shield,' Mekki explained. 'It now points into the shelter, rather than out.'

'You've trapped it inside the dome,' Zelia realised.

Mekki nodded proudly. 'Like a caged animal.'

'But can't it just rip down the wires?' Talen asked.

'No, because they're now protected by the force field,' Zelia said. 'It's brilliant.'

The alien raged inside the dome, throwing Talen's bunk at the wall. Then it stopped and glared at them through the jagged tear, its chest heaving.

'Don't look at its eyes,' Zelia said, turning away.

Talen's hand went to his belt. He looked up in horror and saw the pouch containing his toy soldier lying on the floor next to Scarface's feet. The Genestealer's eyes narrowed and it looked down at the leather bag. It reached down and slowly picked up the pouch with one of its five-fingered hands.

'No!' shouted Talen. 'Leave that alone.'

Scarface looked up and held out the pouch in a purple-skinned hand. Without thinking, Talen stepped forwards, locking eyes with the creature.

'Talen, no. Not again.' Zelia grabbed Talen and pulled him away before he could be caught in another trance.

'But my pouch...'

She forced him to look at her. 'Would your brother have wanted you to go in there and get it? What would he say if he were here?'

Talen turned away, pulling his coat around him. He knew she was right.

Inside the shelter, the Genestealer growled, throwing the pouch to the floor in fury.

'We cannot stay here,' Mekki told them. 'The cells have maybe twenty minutes of power left.'

Zelia faced him, trying to ignore the sound of a Genestealer tearing the inside of their temporary home apart. 'The technology Fleapit's been finding.

Do we think it's a ship?'

Mekki nodded. 'It is a distinct possibility.'

'What are you thinking?' Talen asked.

'I'm thinking that we need shelter,' Zelia said. 'And we can't go back in there. Fleapit is going to have to take us to the other ship.'

'But monkey-brain is asleep,' Talen reminded her.

'Then we're going to have to wake him up!'

CHAPTER TEN

Memories

To Mekki's relief the blizzard was lifting. While the others had managed to grab their thermo-coats, he had been concentrating on reprogramming the force field.

By the time they reached Flegan-Pala's nest, his teeth were chattering so loudly that he almost couldn't hear the thrashing of the Genestealer in the dome.

'Well, how are we going to wake him?' asked Talen as Zelia shone her lume-rod at the hibernating Jokaero.

She crouched down, shaking the ape's hairy arm.

Outside, the noises from the dome stopped.

The children exchanged a worried glance.

'You think it's gone back down its rabbit hole?' Talen asked.

'There's nothing to stop it,' Zelia said, renewing her attempts to wake the slumbering alien. 'Come on, Fleapit. Please.'

This was getting them nowhere. Mekki reached up, snatching the servo-sprite from where it had been hovering beside him.

Talen peered over his shoulder. 'What are you doing, Cog-Boy?'

'Please do not call me that,' Mekki said, pressing a haptic implant against the robot's back. The tiny robot stiffened as he accessed its machine-spirit. 'Flegan-Pala has a connection to the servo-sprite. Maybe I can use it to reach him.'

He twisted his finger. Images burst across his mind's eye. Mekki gasped as he accessed the servo-sprite's memory wafers, experiencing the data the automaton had gathered from Flegan-Pala. He saw the Necrons' attack on Targian, but not how they had experienced it on the ground. Suddenly, he was up in the spires, at the very top of Rhal Rata where the rich and powerful lived.

He heard Zelia's voice, sounding as if it were a million miles away. 'Mekki? What are you seeing?'

'People are running,' he told her. 'People in fine clothes... Running, screaming, abandoning their grand homes.' He twisted the probe in the servo-sprite's back. 'But not Flegan-Pala.'

'You can see him.'

'These are his memories on the day of the fall.'

'How is this helping?' he heard Talen whisper, only to be hushed by Zelia.

'Go on, Mekki. Tell us what happened to Flea... to Flegan-Pala.'

Mekki winced, the memories difficult

to witness. 'He is shut in a box.'

'A box?'

'No bigger than a storage crate back on the *Scriptor*. He slams his fists on the closed lid. He hears the sounds of explosions and las-fire. He needs to get out. He needs to be free.'

Other images flowed through Mekki's mind. Voices yelling at Flegan-Pala, demanding that he worked harder... faster... A hand slapping down. A hand wearing fine golden rings.

'Mekki?'

The Martian forced himself to describe what he was seeing. 'Flegan-Pala kicks with his feet, the lid flying off... The hive is... rumbling... quaking... The apartment is empty, his masters gone.

'He runs, dodging walls that collapse, leaping over fires that blaze in the corridor. He pushes open the doors of a turbo-lift and clambers down the shaft, down, down, to the middle levels... to the space port.'

'Where we escaped,' Talen said.

Mekki nodded, licking his lips. They were dry, his heart beating fast in time with the frightened Jokaero in the memories.

'He sees someone, a familiar face.'

'Who?'

'It is his master, the man who has enslaved him all these years. He is boarding a ship. Flegan-Pala cries out, racing for the spacecraft. His master turns, sees him running for the ship, and slams the door shut.'

Mekki frowned as he felt the alien's anger, his fear of being left behind after everything he has done for that man.

'The ship launches,' he said, continuing the story. 'A blast of green energy lances across the bay, striking the craft.'

'The Necrons,' Talen muttered.

'The ship explodes, crashing back to the ground. Flegan-Pala looks around, seeing the Necron warriors advance, hearing the chatter of Necron scarabs. There is a voidship.'

'The *Mercator*?' Zelia asked.

Mekki gasped, the connection becoming uncomfortable.

'Mekki?'

'The images are jumping forwards,' he explained. 'Like a dream. It is... disorientating.'

'But is it helping? Are you getting through to him?'

Mekki was lost in the events of the past again. 'I am on the *Mercator*. It is leaving orbit, making the jump to warp space. The Necrons have returned. People are running.' Mekki took a deep intake of breath. 'It is me.'

'You?'

'I can see myself. I can see all of us. Lexmechanic Erasmus getting us into the escape pod, the Ogryn trying to pull us out, Flegan-Pala grabbing the mutant, yanking it back. The pod launching. Crawling into an access hatch. There are colours... confusion. A planet ahead. A crash. Cold, cold air.'

'Mekki, slow down. You're talking too fast.'

The images were coming in a jumble now. *Flegan-Pala wrestling with Talen in the snow. Spotting the Necron Hunter in the forest. Firing the sonic cannon into the trees.*

'Mekki!'

Building the sonic mines. The avalanche. The power flickering. Heading out into the woods, finding metal in the ground.

A hand gripped his wrist and broke the connection, pulling his finger free of the servo-sprite.

Mekki blinked, looking into Zelia's worried face. 'Why did you do that?'

'You were babbling,' she told him. 'We couldn't understand you.'

'Are you all right, Cog-Boy?' Talen was peering at him too, actually looking concerned.

'I asked you not to call me that,' Mekki said quietly.

'And I ignored you. You said something about finding metal. Do you know where Fleapit is finding all the stuff?'

Mekki shook his head. 'The vision was garbled. Confused.'

'It sounded it. Can you at least wake him up?'

'I shall try,' Mekki said, and plugged himself back into the sprite. The robot let out a squeal as Mekki tried to make a connection, but there was nothing. He frowned, letting go of the servo-sprite, which flew to hide behind the Jokaero. 'Flegan-Pala has blocked the connection. I cannot get through to him any more.'

'Fine,' Talen sighed, snatching a bulky power-wrench from the bed of wires. 'If you want something doing, do it yourself...'

'What are you doing?' Zelia gasped as Talen raised the hyper-tool above his head.

'We've tried it your way, now it's time for mine.'

Before she could stop him, Talen brought the wrench down hard, ready to strike Flegan-Pala. The Jokaero's eyes snapped open, and he threw up a hand to block the blow, his long fingers wrapping around the ganger's wrist.

'Ow!' Talen winced.

'Fleapit, you're awake!' Zelia cried.

Mekki almost laughed with relief. 'Flegan-Pala must have a defensive function built into his hibernation program. Of course...'

'Yeah, of course,' Talen repeated, with a sheepish smile.

'How clever of you to work out that

he would wake if attacked, Talen Stormweaver.'

'Yup... clever old me...' the ganger said. 'Now, any chance we can get monkey-features to let go of my wrist?'

With a grunt, Flegan-Pala released him.

Zelia knelt beside the creature. 'Fleapit, I know the cold is hurting you, but we need your help. There's something out there – a Genestealer.'

Flegan-Pala's eyes went wide, and he flashed a look at Mekki.

'It is true,' the Martian told him. 'We have trapped the xenos in the shelter...'

'At least that's where we left it,' added Talen, rubbing his wrist.

Mekki nodded. 'But we cannot stay here. We need to find somewhere to hide.'

'Somewhere like your secret spaceship,' Talen said.

The Jokaero snarled, showing its teeth.

'It's okay,' Zelia said. 'We're not

cross, and we don't want to steal your salvage. You found it and it's yours, but if it can keep us safe from the Genestealer...'

Flegan-Pala considered her words, before grunting in agreement. Mekki felt the connection between their minds open again, a babble of digital information passing between them.

'There is a ship,' he translated for the others, 'buried on the other side of the forest. A very old ship.'

'Can he take us there?' Zelia asked.

Flegan-Pala tried to push himself up from the bed, but his arms were too weak.

'He is not strong enough,' Mekki said.

'He could just point us in the right direction,' Talen suggested.

'We're not leaving him,' Zelia told him.

Putting one of the Jokaero's long arms around her shoulders, Zelia helped him up. Mekki moved in to help, grabbing his other arm. Flegan-Pala was heavy, his joints stiff. His head was already lolling, as if he could barely stay awake.

This wasn't going to be easy.

CHAPTER ELEVEN

Discovery

The walk through the snow was more
difficult than ever. Fleapit was doing
his best, but was slipping in and out
of consciousness. They ended up half
dragging the ape for most of the way.
Their progress wasn't helped by the
fact that Mekki was freezing. The
storm had passed, but he was still only
wearing his Martian robes. His teeth
were permanently chattering and his
lips and nose had turned blue.

Zelia wasn't the only one to notice
his condition. Halfway through their
trudge through the mushroom forest,
Talen stopped, removed his coat and

draped it over Mekki's shoulders. Zelia smiled, the act of kindness speaking volumes.

Talen saw her looking, and indicated his arm in the sling. 'It's not like I can help carry monkey-breath.'

He wasn't fooling anyone.

Fleapit was almost asleep by the time they'd crossed the forest. The servo-sprite buzzed back and forth, unsure which way to go.

'Where now?' Zelia asked, trying to catch her breath.

Talen scanned the ground in front of them. Spotting something, he ran forwards and pulled a length of red metal from the snow.

'There's junk everywhere,' he said, digging another twisted shard of shrapnel from beneath the snow. 'It looks like it's been here a while.'

The giant mushrooms had thinned out, and they were climbing a slight incline, like a dune in the snow. Talen dropped onto his knees and started digging with his good arm. Zelia lowered Fleapit to the ground and ran to help, picking up a length of metal and using it as a shovel.

There was a dull clang beneath the snow.

'Yes!' Talen shouted. 'There's something down here.'

Zelia looked into the hole. They'd uncovered a sheet of scratched red metal.

'That's a hull plate. It's Fleapit's ship.'

Mekki joined in the excavation, scooping up handfuls of snow. Before long they had uncovered a circular hatch. As Zelia and Talen cleared as much snow as they could, Mekki checked for an opening mechanism. When he couldn't find one, Talen reached for the length of metal Zelia had been using to dig.

'What if we use this as a crowbar?' he asked, ramming it beneath the edge of the hatch. He pushed down, his face screwed up against the pain of his shoulder.

'Here, let me,' Zelia said, taking over.
There was a clunk and the hatch
opened slightly. She pushed again, the
servo-sprite trying to peer into the
widening gap, looking for a catch.

The metal started to bend as a howl
echoed through the mushroom-trees.

Talen looked up. 'Scarface.'

The Genestealer must have followed
their scent.

'Help me,' Zelia said, and all three
pushed down on the metal.

The alien's howl was getting nearer.
Zelia could imagine it charging through
the forest, its arms raised and ready to
strike.

The hatch wouldn't budge.

'It's no good,' she grunted.

'No,' Mekki said. 'Look.'

The servo-sprite was wriggling beneath
the hatch.

'What's it doing?' Talen asked as it
squeezed inside the gap they had made.

They heard it flying around inside the

ship. Mekki's electoos glowed as it sent back a report. 'It is searching for the locking mechanism.'

'Can you tell it to hurry up?' asked Talen.

With a deep, reverberating clang, the lock released. The servo-sprite buzzed back out into the frosty air and bobbed around as if expecting applause.

Zelia pulled open the hatch to reveal a shaft dropping down into darkness. She flicked on her lume-rod and shone the light into the opening. There was a ladder, its rungs covered in rust.

'That doesn't look safe,' she commented, but Talen had already slipped his injured arm out of his sling and was clambering into the shaft.

'I'd rather take my chances with a rusty old ladder than tackle Scarface again,' he said, wincing as he started the climb down.

'What about Fleapit?' she asked.

There was a grunt from behind and she turned to see Fleapit dragging

himself towards her.
Mekki helped the
Jokaero onto the ladder
and then followed him
down into the shaft.

'A little light would
be nice,' Talen called
up from below.

Zelia handed the
lume-rod to the sprite.
It gripped the torch in
both hands and flew
down to light the way.

Zelia stepped onto the
ladder, feeling the rung
give slightly beneath
her foot. She climbed
down a few steps and
reached up to pull the
hatch over her head.

'What are you waiting
for?' Talen shouted up.

'It's stuck,' she said,
pulling hard. She
couldn't move it.

Zelia looked up to see Scarface burst out of the trees and run straight for them, claws raised.

The ship

CHAPTER TWELVE

The Ship

The Genesteaeler threw up plumes of snow as it charged towards them, using its remaining arms to propel itself faster and faster. Zelia tugged at the hatch, but it still wouldn't budge. She daren't look up, knowing what would happen if she made eye contact with the monster. The others were calling her name, screaming at her to close the airlock. As if she wasn't trying! She could hear the guttural snarl of the alien, feel its foul breath on her neck.

'Come on,' she shouted as she pulled with all her might. 'Why. Won't. You. Close!'

The Genestealer leapt at her – and the hatch slammed shut. The sudden movement made Zelia slip and she stepped heavily onto a tread that was almost completely devoured by rust. The corroded metal snapped, and she tumbled down the shaft.

She grabbed out, finding another rung. Her body slammed back into the ladder.

'Zelia?' Talen was already climbing back up to check on her.

'I'm fine,' she breathed, resting her forehead against the metal before scrabbling sounds made her head snap up. The Genestealer was trying to claw its way in.

The others were waiting for her at the bottom of the shaft. They were crammed into a space no larger than her closet on the *Scriptor*, the only light coming from the lume-rod held by the jittery servo-sprite.

'How do we get out of here?' she asked, stepping off the ladder.

'There is a door,' Mekki said, 'but no

power to open it.'

Talen tried to force it open. 'It's no good,' he grunted. 'My shoulder...'

'Let me help,' Zelia said, and between them they managed to slide the door back enough for Fleapit to slip his long fingers into the crack. Baring his teeth, the Jokaero slid the door into the wall and the children stepped through, emerging into a long, dark corridor.

Zelia took her torch from the sprite and shone it up and down the corridor. Doors lined either side, the walls covered in a thin layer of ice while glittering icicles hung from the ceiling like witches' fingers. The deck plates were slippery, but at least the floor was reasonably level. The ship had come to rest on a slight angle, but not enough to give them trouble standing.

'Any chance of a hand?' Talen asked, trying to drag Fleapit out of the shaft. The Jokaero had slumped back into his hibernation.

They leant him against the wall as

Mekki brushed frost from a cogitator terminal and found an access point compatible with his haptic implants.

With a hum, lume-strips flickered on near their feet, the spooky, low-level lighting casting strange shadows along the corridor.

'There's power?' Talen asked.

'Emergency power,' Mekki corrected him. He twisted his fingers in the access ports and the door to the shaft shut with a satisfying click.

'But that means we might be able

to get things working?' Zelia asked hopefully.

'Like the heating?' Talen added, trying to rub some warmth into his arms.

Mekki nodded. 'In theory, yes.' He continued to probe the cogitator. 'But not from here. We would need to find the enginarium.'

'Could we take off?' Zelia asked.

'Possibly,' Mekki replied. 'But that would depend on the damage. At the very least, the armoured hull would provide better protection than our camp.'

'So, we could wait here to be rescued.'

Mekki disconnected his fingers from the cogitator. 'And of course, the vox-transmitters on a ship this size will be more powerful than our beacon. We may be able to contact the *Scriptor*.'

Zelia's heart leapt at the mention of her mother's ship. She was sure Elise was still out there, waiting for her. *Meet at the Emperor's Seat*, her mum had said during their last transmission

– wherever that was.

'What about our friend up there?' Talen asked, pointing at the ceiling.

'The outer hull is constructed of reinforced ceramite,' Mekki told him. 'Nothing can cut through it.'

'And you're sure about that?' Talen asked.

The Martian didn't answer.

Talen shook his head. 'Well, that's just brilliant.'

'We just have to hope that he can't get in,' Zelia said.

'*Hope*? Is that it?'

Zelia shrugged. 'What else do we have?'

Talen sighed. 'Well, something to eat would be good. Reckon there's any food down here?'

'There could be dry rations,' Mekki suggested. 'The ship has obviously been here a long time, but some supplies may still be edible.'

'Then I'll go look for them,' said Talen.

Mekki frowned. 'Where will you look?'

Talen grinned. 'I'll just follow my stomach.'

'Well, at least we know the engines are likely to be near the rear of the ship,' Zelia said, pointing behind them with her lume-rod.

Talen narrowed his eyes. 'How?'

She shrugged. 'Basic starship design. Engines are usually at the back.'

He blushed in the low light. 'Oh yeah... Sorry.'

'Don't apologise,' she told him, clicking off the lume-rod and slipping it back into her bandolier. 'We're all out of our depth here.'

He raised his eyebrows. 'Even you?'

'Even me,' she admitted. 'But I've picked up a few things working with mum. In all the large ships we've excavated, the refectory is usually pretty central.'

'Refectory?'

'Where the food is. I'll show you.' She started towards a bend in the corridor ahead.

'No,' Talen said quickly. 'You should go with Mekki.'

'But you're hurt.'

He flexed his shoulder, trying not to wince. 'I'm fine, honestly. And I'm no good at all that techy stuff. You're the one who spent her life on starships. Me?' He tapped his midriff. 'I grew up following my stomach.'

'Are you sure?'

'Absolutely.' His tone told her that he wasn't in the mood to argue. After the business with the Ambull, Talen needed to do this... and she needed to let him.

'You have your vox-box?'

He tapped his belt. 'Right where it should be...'

Unlike your pouch, Zelia thought, knowing how much it meant to him.

Talen nodded at Fleapit, who was still slumped against the wall. 'What about snooze-bag?'

Zelia bit her lip. 'I don't fancy dragging him all the way to the enginarium.'

'But what if we leave him here and the Genestealer gets in?' Mekki pointed out.

Zelia walked over to a door on the other side of the corridor. 'What's in here?'

Mekki tapped the cogitator and the door opened to reveal a small cabin.

'That's perfect,' Zelia said. 'Fleapit should be safe in here until we can get the heating working.'

'*If* we can get the heating working,' Mekki corrected her, and they grabbed the alien's long arms and hauled him into the cabin.

'He doesn't get any lighter, does he?' she complained, as they rested the Jokaero on a bunk and shut the door. Zelia reached beneath her coat and pulled out her lume-rod. 'Here,' she said, handing it to Talen. 'You better take this, in case the lights go out.'

He took it gratefully, slipping the torch into his jacket. 'Just try to make sure that doesn't happen, yeah?'

'We will do our best,' Mekki replied.

Talen gave the Martian an embarrassed smile. 'That's good enough for me. Look, what I said earlier, about you not being up to the job...'

Mekki responded by removing the coat Talen had given him. 'We both said things we regret, Talen Stormweaver.'

Talen held up his good hand to stop him. 'You keep it.'

Mekki rewarded the ganger with a rare smile. 'Just be careful.'

'You too, Cog-Boy,' Talen said, heading off down the corridor. 'Look after Zelia.'

'We'll look after *each other*,' she called after him as he disappeared around the corner.

'Right,' she said, turning to face Mekki. 'Let's find those engines.'

As they walked in silence, Zelia told herself that it was going to be all right. So they'd seen the Genestealer make short work of their shelter, and even claw through rock, but the armoured hull of a space cruiser was something else. Soon it would give up and scuttle back to wherever it had come from.

Yeah, she was sure of that.

Of course, she didn't see the tip of a long, purple claw pierce the hatch at the top of the access shaft, or hear the squeal of metal as it sliced the door in two.

CHAPTER THIRTEEN

In the Shadows

'There's nothing to worry about,' Talen told himself, as he walked deeper into the buried ship. 'You can do tunnels. Tunnels are good. Nothing bad's going to happen...'

Other than the ceiling suddenly collapsing on him, or the emergency lights failing, or slipping on the icy floor and knocking himself out...

The labyrinthine corridors seemed to be closing in as he searched from room to room. He knew that it was only claustrophobia setting in, as was the nagging doubt that he was lost. He made himself continue, following the slight slope of the floor that forced him to tread carefully, using the power lines that ran along the wall as a rail to stop himself from slipping.

The trouble was that all the corridors looked the same, and most of the doors wouldn't open. They either needed power to operate, or their mechanisms were frozen by a combination of ice and rust.

Talen wanted to open his vox and ask Zelia and Mekki what was taking so long. He needed proper light. He needed *heat* – especially after giving away his coat. His hand went to the vox-box on his belt, but he stopped himself. He didn't want them to hear the apprehension in his voice.

Ahead of him, the lume-strips along the floor were spluttering, each flicker accompanied by the fizz of sparking electricity. The entire section of corridor was strobing, the lights snapping on and off. Talen took a deep breath and pushed on, focusing on the next section, where the lights were strong.

'It's just a loose connection,' he muttered to himself. 'There's nothing to be afraid of.'

That didn't stop him from crying out when the light gave out completely, plunging the entire section into darkness. He broke into a run, nearly skidding as he raced towards the light, and only stopped when he was back in the soft glow of the lume-strips.

'Stupid,' he scolded himself as he forced himself to breathe. 'It was dark, that's all.'

Something scraped behind him.

Talen turned and peered into the gloom.

It was probably nothing, just the deck plates creaking after being disturbed for the first time in years. Still, his hands were shaking as he pulled out Zelia's lume-rod and shone a light into the darkness.

He swept the beam back and forth. Everything was as it should be, the cables on the walls and the locked doors. There was nothing waiting for him in the shadows. He must have imagined it.

And then the light swept past something in the gloom, something crouched near the floor. Leathery skin. Snarling jaws. A scarred, pupilless eye.

The Genestealer bounded towards him.

It had got in. It had cut through the hatch and scrambled down the shaft, and now it was here, chasing Talen down the corridor. So much for Mekki's ceramite. So much for Zelia's hope. Talen hoped he'd live long enough to say he'd told them so.

No, scratch that. He just wanted to live.

He ran, not caring about the ice beneath his feet. Behind him, Scarface snarled and hissed, its claws clattering on the frozen deck.

Talen slid around the corner to find his path blocked by a heavy door. He pressed a button, praying there would be enough power. The door started to swish open, before jamming halfway. Talen didn't have time to wait. He squeezed through the gap, before turning to force the door shut again. The mechanism squealed, but the door moved, sliding back into place.

Talen jumped back as two of Scarface's claws slammed through the gap, stopping the door from shutting.

He kicked at the claws, but they didn't retract. He lashed out again, this time kicking the door control. The panel sparked, locking the door in place.

Talen ran, knowing that the barrier wouldn't hold for long. He tried the doors leading off from the corridor, but they were all locked. There was nowhere to hide.

Behind him, Scarface pounded at the door, knocking dents into the metal.

At the other end of the ship, unaware of Talen's panic, Zelia and Mekki had found what they were looking for. The ship's enginarium was huge, giant turbines lined up one after the other. Lume-globes glowed weakly in the high vaulted ceiling, the emergency power unable to light such a large area. Once, this would have been a hive of activity, enginseers rushing from turbine to turbine making sure everything was running properly. Now the enormous generators were silent and covered in ice.

'What do you think happened to the crew?' Zelia asked as Mekki pulled

up a chair in front of a large control console.

'The ship is old,' he said, flicking switches. 'They will be long gone.'

She dropped into the seat next to him, hugging herself against the cold. 'Yes, but we've dug up enough ships to know that there are always remains – spacesuits, or uniforms.'

'Not to mention skeletons.'

'Exactly.' The thought was ghoulish, but Mekki was right. And yet here, there was nothing. The ship was simply deserted.

Not that Mekki cared. He had already patched himself into the cogitator. As long as there was a machine to talk to, the Martian didn't need a crew.

Zelia knew what *she* needed – heat! She half wished she could follow Fleapit's example and put herself into a hibernation cycle. The cold felt as if it had got into her bones. Her hands were numb, and she couldn't feel her feet. Zelia's mum had once introduced her to an explorator who had excavated an old temple on the frozen wastes of Ricardia. Zelia had taken one look at the cybernetic digits on his hands, and asked the old man what had happened to his real fingers.

'Frostbite,' the grizzled explorator had told her, wiggling the mechanical replacements at her. 'Woke up one morning to discover that they'd dropped off, just like that.'

The thought had haunted Zelia for years, and sitting here in the bitter enginarium she fought the urge to count her own fingers just to make sure they were still where they should be.

'Can you get the engines started?' Zelia asked, anything to stop her thoughts of blackened hands and toes.

'Possibly.' With a flick of his hand, Mekki sent the servo-sprite to examine the turbines. 'They have been dormant for many years, but...'

He let his words hang in the air as

he worked the console like a musical instrument.

'But what?' Zelia asked, her teeth chattering.

In response, every screen on the console flickered into life, cogitator glyphs scrolling up the display. The lume-globes pulsed above their heads and the turbines started to whirr.

Zelia clapped her hands together. 'Mekki. You're doing it. You're a genius!'

The Martian allowed himself the slightest of smiles as he scanned the glyphs on the screens.

'Yes,' he said quietly. 'Yes, I am.'

CHAPTER FOURTEEN

The Grav-Gun

'Hello? Zelia? Mekki? Are you there?'

Talen fumbled with the vox-box, his hands cramping with the cold. They were so numb that he couldn't even open a channel to call for help. He shoved the vox back into a pocket on his vest. What did he expect the others to do anyway? They were probably at the other side of the ship by now, and if Scarface was following him, at least it wasn't tracking them.

The thought made him laugh. Talen the self-sacrificing hero. Who would have thought it? Definitely not him.

But he couldn't stay here, hiding in

the dark.

Lights flashed on above his head. Okay. Not in the dark any more. He put a hand against the wall, feeling a faint vibration through the metal. The ship had power. They'd done it. Maybe they'd find a way to take off, if the damage wasn't too great. He had to give them more time, and if that meant keeping the Genestealer busy, so be it.

By the sound of tearing metal, it wouldn't be long until Scarface came after him. He had to hide. He tried some of the doors along the corridor, but even with the renewed power, they refused to open.

There had to be somewhere he could go.

Something cold splashed onto his cheek. He looked up. The ice that covered the low ceiling was melting to reveal a series of square grates running down the middle of the passageway. He squinted. Was there something above them? A ventilation shaft or access

tunnel? Whatever it was, Talen knew
an escape route when he saw one.

He ran along the corridor until
he found a ladder leading up to an
access hatch. Ignoring the ache in his
shoulder, he clambered up, pushing the
hatch open and seeing that he was
right. It was a pipe, stuffed with cables
and circuit boards, but with enough
space to crawl through. Maybe he could
escape Scarface after all. If these pipes
ran the length of the ship, he could
use them to get to the others. Together
they'd find a way of stopping the
Genestealer. They had before, and this
time they had an entire ship at their
disposal.

Either way, he couldn't stay here.
The temperature was rising, the air in
the pipe already stifling. Carefully, he
closed the hatch behind him. Would the
Genestealer work out where he had
gone? No, the monster was nothing
more than a dumb animal. There was
no way Scarface could follow him. It

would stalk the corridors, unable to find him, unaware that he was crawling above its stupid purple head.

He started along the corridor, hauling himself forwards on his elbows and knees. His shoulder burned, but that was nothing to the pain he would feel if Scarface caught up with him. Within seconds he was drenched in sweat. It dropped through the grille, adding to the drip, drip, drip of the melting ice on the floor below. And to think that he'd wanted it to be hotter!

Something clanged behind him and Talen's heart sank. That had come from the pipe, and could only mean one thing. The Genestealer was breaking into the shaft. So much for dumb animals. The ganger sped up, ignoring the pain from the elbows he was grazing against the grille. The sound of scraping talons filled the shaft. Yup, the Genestealer was in the pipe all right. It was scrabbling after him. The thought of being cornered in such a confined space made him feel sick, but surely the size of the pipe had to work to his advantage. Talen only just fitted into the shaft. The Genestealer would be too big. At the very least, it would be slowed down. Talen could hear the creature's claws scraping as it dragged itself along. He couldn't relax. Back home he had seen huge sewer rats squeeze through the tiniest of gaps. For all he knew, the Genestealer could do the same.

Talen passed another pipe that jutted

off to the left. Should he continue on or wriggle around the bend? Either way the Genestealer would probably follow him by scent alone. He was certainly sweating enough.

Taking his chances, he turned left, hoping he wasn't heading towards a dead end. He looked down and realised that he was crawling across a room, and not just any room at that. Racks lined the wall, each holding row after row of weaponry. It was an armoury!

Pulling up the grille panel in front of him, Talen dropped down to the floor. He stretched, his spine cracking after being cooped up. The grille was still open above him and he had no way to close it from down here, but it didn't matter. If Scarface found him now, at least he would be ready.

Talen headed straight for the lasgun racks. He tried to pull one of the rifles free from its clip, but found it was locked in place. He pulled harder, rattling the weapon in the rack, but there was no way to get it free.

He could hear grunting from above. Scarface was closing in fast. He moved to a set of drawers next to the door. Like the beamers, most of the weapons inside were locked down, the clamps rusted with age. He was running out of time. There must be something he could use to defend himself.

He got lucky with the third drawer he opened, finding a chunky pistol. It was clamped down, but as he peered closer he could see a hairline crack in the

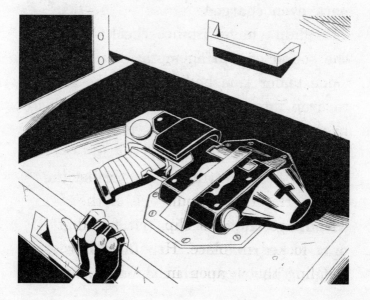

restraint. He wriggled the weapon, and the crack widened until finally he could pull the pistol free. It was surprisingly light for its size, even with a power pack in its grip. He held it out, peering down its sights as he aimed at the wall. Back on Targian, he'd carried an ancient beamer on his hip, an antique weapon stolen from his father on the day he ran away from home. It had only been for show and had never really worked. For all he knew, the pistol was also a dud. Was the power pack even charged?

He didn't have time to check. With the sound of tearing metal, the Genestealer smashed through the grille to drop into the armoury. It landed in front of Talen and hissed through pointed teeth. Talen didn't hesitate. Raising a shaking hand, he pulled the trigger.

Nothing happened. He tried again, only to be rewarded with the same result. The trigger clicked but didn't fire. The pistol was useless.

The Genestealer snarled in triumph.
Its prey was trapped and defenceless.
It pounced at the exact moment
Talen noticed a switch on the back
of the cylinder. He flicked it with his
thumb and fired one last time. A bolt
of brilliant blue light burst from the
pistol, hitting Scarface in the chest.
The alien flew across the armoury and
landed on its back. The Genestealer
snarled and growled, its limbs glowing
with blue energy, but didn't leap back
to its feet. It lay there, struggling but
unable to move, as if held down by a
great weight.

Talen stared at the pistol in his
hands. What was this thing? Some kind
of force field generator, like Fleapit's
webbing back at the shelter, pinning
its victim in place? Whatever it was, it
had worked better than he could have
hoped. The Genestealer wailed in fury.
Talen fought an urge to look into its
eyes. He wasn't going to let himself be

hypnotised again.

Turning his back on the alien, he pressed the button to open the armoury door. The control beeped, but the door remained locked. He tried again, and a tinny computerised voice issued from a speaker-grille.

'Input passcode.'

'What?' Talen spluttered. 'What kind of door needs a code to get out? Codes are to stop people getting in.'

'Unauthorised use of weapon detected,' the cogitator replied. 'The armourium has been sealed for the protection of the crew.'

'The crew's gone,' he told it. 'I'm the one that needs protecting.'

'Please input passcode to exit.'

'But I don't have a passcode!' Talen yelled.

Behind him, the Genestealer shifted on the floor. Was the blue beam wearing off? He couldn't risk turning around to check.

Talen snatched the vox-box from his

belt. 'Zelia? Mekki? Come in please. I could really do with some help.'

He took his finger off the button and waited. There was no answer.

'Zelia,' he said, trying again. 'Mekki. Where are you?'

In the enginarium, Zelia felt like a spare part. The turbines were roaring, the servo-sprite darting between the generators, while Mekki was plugged into the console muttering away to himself in that strange binaric language of his. Glyphs scrolled across the cogitator displays as the Martian studied the ship's systems one by one.

At least she could check in on Talen. She activated the vox on her sleeve.

'Talen? How are you getting on? Have you found anything?'

There was no response.

'The ship's superstructure is interfering with our vox signals,' Mekki told her without even looking up from the screens.

She let her arm drop back down.
'Well, is there a ship-wide vox-system?'
she asked. 'Something I can use to talk
to Talen?'

He leant across her and activated a
control. 'Hold down the red button to
speak,' he said, returning to his display.

'Which one?' she asked, looking down
at the console. 'There are loads of red
buttons.'

Mekki didn't reply, lost in a
private conversation with the ship's
machine-spirit.

'Never mind,' she said, pressing the
buttons at random. 'Hello? Talen, can
you hear me?'

Zelia's voice boomed around the empty
corridors of the crashed space cruiser,
echoing out of every vox-caster.

In the armourium, Talen searched
desperately for the voice control on the
panel in front of him.

'Talen, come in please. Talen?'

'Yeah, I hear you.'

Behind him, the blue glow around Scarface's limbs was fading. The Genestealer hissed as it discovered it could flex its fingers.

'Talen?'

'Yes,' Talen snapped, pressing a button. 'I'm here. You need to open the door.'

'What?' Zelia asked over the vox-channel.

'I'm trapped in a room with the Genestealer and would really like to get out.'

'The Genestealer's in the ship?'

'No, I'm joking,' he snarled, before yelling: 'OPEN THE DOOR!'

Mekki's clipped voice came over the vox. 'Where are you, Talen Stormweaver?'

'In some kind of armoury.'

'On which deck?'

'How am I supposed to know? There are a lot of weapons and one very angry alien. Just get me out of here.'

Behind him, Scarface struggled against the blue beam before collapsing back on the floor. Talen turned and, trying not to look into the alien's eyes, blasted it again just in case.

'*What was that?*' Zelia asked through the vox.

'I found a pistol. It's trapped Scarface in some kind of bubble, weighing him down.'

'*You mean like a gravity field?*' Mekki asked.

'If you say so. But I've no idea how long it'll last, or how many shots I've got left.'

There was the sound of buttons being pressed. '*Stand by,*' Mekki told him.

'What do you *think* I'm doing?'

'*Passcode accepted,*' the cogitator announced, and the door slid open.

'Thank you,' Talen breathed and darted outside, slapping the controls as soon as he was in the corridor. The door slid shut. Talen found a vox-panel on the wall.

'Mekki, can you lock that thing inside the room?'

'*Of course,*' the Martian said, as if the answer was obvious.

'*Door locked,*' said the cogitator.

Talen looked down the corridor. Water was dripping from the ceiling as the ice continued to melt.

'Guess you got the heating working,' he said into the air, wondering which way to go.

'*Mekki's working wonders back here,*' Zelia replied. '*Did you find any food?*'

'Before or after I was attacked?'

'*Sorry. Wasn't thinking. Are you all right?*'

'Yeah, but I don't want to stay around here.'

'*Can you find your way back here?*'

'It would help if I knew where I was.' He turned and looked the other way down the corridor. 'This is hopeless. Back home, I could find my way through any tunnel system. There was always something to guide me – moss on the pipes, airflow. Here, nothing makes sense. It's all so... artificial.'

'You're doing great. Better *than* great. If it had been me down there, I'd be... well, I don't want to think what I'd be. Hang on, I'll see if I can find you a map.'

Once again, there was a clatter of keys.

'Anytime soon would be good.'

There was a thump against the armoury door. The gravity field had worn off.

'Actually, scratch that, I'll find my own way,' Talen shouted over his shoulder as he broke into a run. 'Scarface is back on his feet.'

The Genestealer's claws sliced through the door as if it were paper.

CHAPTER FIFTEEN

Beneath the Ice

In the enginarium, Zelia turned to Mekki. 'We need a map of the ship.'

The Martian didn't reply.

'Mekki, did you hear me? Talen is in trouble. I need to guide him back.'

The pale-skinned boy was staring ahead, finger-probes jammed into the computer ports, eyes glazed over.

'Accessing records,' he said, his voice dreamlike. 'Security officer's log.'

'Will that help with the map?' Zelia asked, hopefully.

When Mekki replied, his voice wasn't his own. It sounded deeper, older.

'Systems are shutting down all over

the ship... Damage on all decks...'

'Mekki?'

'Sabotage cannot be ruled out...'

Zelia realised what was happening. The Martian's eyes were misted over, the electoos on his skin flashing.

'Mekki, is this a report from before the crash? Is this what happened to the crew?'

'They're everywhere...' Mekki shouted in another voice, higher this time. 'Swarming through the ship. Too many of them.'

'Too many of what?' she asked.

Another voice spilled out of Mekki. 'This is the captain. We're going down. All hands, abandon ship. Repeat, all hands–'

Mekki cried out, arching his back as if experiencing the crash for himself. He pulled his fingers from the computer and slumped back in the chair.

'Mekki?' Zelia said, touching his arm. He flinched as if burned.

'It's all right,' she said hurriedly, 'it's

just me. You're safe.'

'No,' Mekki stammered. 'No, I am not. None of us are.'

'Why?'

He grasped her arm. His hand was shaking. 'I know why the ship crashed. The crew tried to fight back, but there were too many of them.'

'Too many of what?' she asked, fear twisting her gut as she guessed what he was going to say.

'Genestealers,' he replied, gravely. 'Dozens of Genestealers.'

Talen was really lost this time.

He had taken a wrong turn and ended up in a maze of corridors. They were in a bad state, the walls blackened, as if there had been a fire long ago. Cables hung down from the ceiling in clumps, the access shafts above exposed. Electrics fizzed and sparked, the lume-strips flicking on and off. It was like something out of a nightmare. From the slope of the floor he could tell he was near the front of the ship. Was this damage from the crash, or something else? Some of the scorch marks looked like las-burns. What had happened down here?

He found a comm-panel and activated a channel.

'Zelia, any luck with that map? I don't know where I am.' She didn't answer. 'Zelia, are you there?'

Maybe the vox-system wasn't working this far down. And if he couldn't hear the others, they couldn't hear him. He was on his own.

A noise from behind made him jump. Was that the Genestealer? He spun around, grav-gun in hand. There was nothing there. Not yet.

Talen backed around the corner and nearly tumbled into a gaping hole in the deck. He reached out, grabbing a power cable to stop himself falling. The floor must have collapsed into the deck below. None of the lights were working in this section. Talen had no way to continue. He'd have to go back.

Something moved in the pit. Talen scrabbled for Zelia's lume-rod, shining the torch into the hole. A face glared back at him, razor-sharp fangs glinting in the light of his beam. Talen cried out, before realising that the Genestealer wasn't moving. It was trapped beneath a sheet of ice, and it wasn't alone. There were dozens down there, long limbs wrapped around their frozen bodies as if they were asleep.

No, not asleep. Like Fleapit. They

were *hibernating*.

Then what had moved?

He swept the light across the frozen Genestealers, noticing a fissure in the ice. Is that where Scarface had come from? And how had he worked himself out?

Talen cried out as something cold splashed onto his neck. The lume-rod slipped from his fingers and tumbled into the hole. It clattered onto the ice.

Talen wiped his neck, his fingers coming back wet. It was just water from ice thawing on the ceiling.

The thought made his breath catch in his throat.

If the ice on the ceiling was melting, then what about the ice in the hole?

There was a crack from below. Talen looked down to see the figures in the ice starting to stir, their limbs uncurling and claws twitching.

The ice was melting. They were waking up!

Talen turned and ran for his life.

CHAPTER SIXTEEN

Trapped

'Talen, can you hear me?'

Zelia shouted into her wrist-vox as she ran down the corridor with Mekki, the servo-sprite darting ahead. Mekki had patched their vox-boxes into the ship's system before they'd left the enginarium, not that it was doing much good. Talen wasn't answering, and they had no idea where he was. All they could do was run to his last known location. Of course that could mean running into Scarface, but that was a risk they'd just have to take.

If Scarface had come down with the ship, surviving the crash for so long there was every chance that the rest of the Genestealers had survived as well. She knew from what her mother had told her that the aliens could live for hundreds of years, lying in wait for their next victims.

She had thought coming to the ship would keep them safe, but she'd been wrong. If the Genestealers were alive, they were in more danger than ever before.

She tried her vox again. 'Talen, please... come in.'

'Zelia?'

'Talen,' she cried out in relief. 'Where are you?'

I've no idea, but I've got a horrible feeling I'm going around in circles. We've got company down here.

She flashed a look at Mekki. 'More Genestealers?'

Yup, and they're waking up. Any chance you could turn down the heating?

Mekki stopped by an access panel

on the wall and attempted to connect himself to the ship's cogitator.

'Not from here,' he admitted. 'We would have to go back to the enginarium.'

'You're not there?' Talen asked over the vox.

'We were coming to find you,' Zelia said.

'It's a warren down here. You'll only get lost yourselves. Just get off the ship.'

'We're not leaving you.'

'You have to. If those things get out of the ice...'

'I get it – we're dead. We'll just have to go back to the engine room and turn off the heating.'

'If you're not already there, it's already too late for that. You go. I'll find another way out,' he told them.

'You said you were lost,' Mekki reminded him.

There was no reply.

'Talen?'

The lume-light flickered.

'The engines are failing,' Mekki said.

'Then how are we going to find Talen?'

All Talen could hear was claws against metal. He didn't want to think how many Genestealers were chasing him. He'd made the mistake of glancing behind after the vox had cut out and had seen a horde of the creatures charging after him. Some were running along the floor, while others were scuttling across the ceiling like spiders.

He turned, firing a couple of blasts from the grav-gun. The first went wide, but the second hit one of the Genestealers on the ceiling. It dropped like a stone, pinning another of the aliens to the floor.

'Two for the price of one,' he muttered to himself as he carried on running.

The main lights flickered and died, plunging the corridor into a split second of complete darkness before the emergency lumes flared on.

The Genestealers were closing in.

He raced around a corner to find his path blocked by an all-too-familiar figure.

Scarface hissed as Talen skidded to a halt. The ganger snapped up the grav-gun but the three-armed Genestealer didn't pounce. Instead it dragged its foot forwards, its knees buckling as if the Genestealer couldn't take the weight of its own body. Talen laughed out loud as blue light glittered around the alien's joints.

It was still affected by the gravity beam.

Talen dodged to the left, squeezing past the monster. Scarface tried to grab him but couldn't move fast enough. Talen ducked beneath the Genestealer's claws and ran on.

Behind him, the rest of the horde tore around the corner. Talen glanced over his shoulder, expecting them to stop in front of Scarface, but instead the aliens ploughed straight through the stricken Genestealer, mowing it down with their claws.

If they did that to one of their own, Talen didn't want to think about what they'd do to him. He hurtled down the corridor, turning a corner to run headlong into a closed door.

'Oh, come on!' he shouted out as he crashed to the floor, dropping the grav-gun. He snatched for the weapon and jumped back to his feet, slamming the door control.

The door refused to open. This

time there was no beep, no annoying cogitator voice – just a solid metal slab that wasn't going anywhere.

He whirled around at the first hiss behind him, raising the grav-gun. The corridor was filled with Genestealers. They had stopped running. What was the point? He had nowhere to go.

He shot once, hitting the nearest Genestealer. He shifted his aim, but his arm suddenly felt like lead. It dropped to his side, the grav-gun loose in his fingers.

He couldn't move, trapped not by a gravity beam but the hypnotic stare of dozens of hungry Genestealers.

CHAPTER SEVENTEEN

The Way Out

A hand dropped down from the ceiling
and grabbed hold of Talen's jacket. It
pulled him up before the Genestealers
could attack, their hooked claws swiping
harmlessly against the door.

Talen found himself dragged into the
shaft above the corridor. He looked up
to see a furry orange face grunting
with the effort of hauling him to safety.

'Fleapit?' he said, still in a daze.
'You're awake.'

In answer, the Jokaero shot out a
long arm and snatched the grav-gun
from his hand.

'Hey!'

Fleapit fired a volley of blue blasts down into the corridor, trapping one Genestealer after another.

'Not bad,' Talen said, genuinely impressed.

The Jokaero gave him a shove, propelling him up the narrow channel.

'Watch who you're pushing,' Talen complained before realising why the ape wanted him to move. The Genestealers were clambering up the walls, climbing over each other to claw at the grilles. He turned and crawled for his life, Fleapit following, blasting the Genestealers that had already made it into the pipe.

'Mekki, what are you doing? Talen is in trouble.'

Zelia went to pull the Martian from the cogitator terminal.

'Wait,' he said, raising his free hand to stop her. 'I have found a map. Uploading.'

'Uploading where?'

Her omniscope beeped. Zelia pulled it out and stared in amazement as a holomap projected from its lens.

'Did you do that?' she asked.

'Maybe Flegan-Pala is not the only miracle worker after all,' Mekki said, pointing at a dot on the three-dimensional map. 'This is Talen Stormweaver's last known location.'

'And this is us?' she asked, pointing at another dot towards the back of the ship.

'Correct.' He leant over and adjusted the focus, and the map zoomed in to show a path through the corridors.

They started running in the direction of Talen's dot, the map bobbing in the air in front of them. Zelia just hoped they weren't too late.

Suddenly, new dots appeared on the hololith, just ahead of them on the map. 'What are they?' Zelia asked.

'The omniscope has detected new life forms.'

Zelia looked ahead. The corridor itself

was empty. 'Where?' she asked.

There was a scrabbling from above. Zelia looked up to see fragments of melting ice dropping down from the channel that ran along the middle of the ceiling. There was the sound of a weapon firing, and the grate in front of them collapsed.

Talen crashed down from the ceiling to land awkwardly on the floor. He clutched his shoulder as she helped him up.

'Where did you come from?'

'A friend dropped in to help me.'

Fleapit leapt down to land nimbly beside them, a curved beamer clutched in one of his simian hands. Zelia went to hug the Jokaero, but he pushed her away rudely.

'Sorry,' she said, nearly dropping the omniscope. 'I'm just glad to see you awake.'

'So the ape gets a hug, but not me?' complained Talen.

'Did you want one?' Zelia asked.

He shook his head. 'No – besides, we haven't time.'

With a hiss, a Genestealer appeared above them. Fleapit fired, encasing the alien in a strange blue light. The Genestealer stiffened and then tumbled down to the floor, where it lay still.

'I assume that is your grav-gun,' Mekki observed.

'You can have a look later,' Talen said, pushing him back up the corridor as Genestealers spilled out of the hole in the ceiling.

The children ran, Fleapit blasting as many Genestealers as possible.

'Where are we going?' Zelia cried out. 'The access shaft is back that way.'

'You're the one with the map,' Talen replied. 'You tell me.'

Mekki tapped his wrist-screen and a new dot appeared on the holomap. 'There.'

'But that will lead us to the side of the ship,' Zelia said.

'Trust me,' Mekki said.

'Do we have a choice?' Talen pointed out.

With Fleapit having far too much fun firing the grav-gun, Zelia guided them through the bowels of the ship.

Soon they reached their destination, a large armourglass airlock at the end of a corridor. There was nowhere else to go but outside.

'But isn't that just rock out there?' Zelia asked.

'Look outside,' Mekki told them.

She rushed up to the window, wiping

grime from the glass. 'It's the caves beneath the forest.'

Mekki was already working on the opening mechanism. 'I saw some of the crew escaping into the tunnels in the ship's logs.'

'And did the crew survive?' Talen asked.

Mekki didn't answer.

'Actually,' the ganger said, 'I don't want to know. Just open the door.'

'The lock is jammed.'

Genestealers piled down the corridor towards them, illuminated by blasts from Fleapit's grav-gun.

'So we're trapped?' Talen asked.

Huffing, Fleapit turned and slapped the grav-gun into Zelia's hand.

'What are you doing?' she said, as the Jokaero grabbed hold of the airlock and ripped it from its hinges.

Talen's jaw dropped open. 'Somebody's feeling better after their nap.'

Fleapit turned and threw the door down the corridor like a giant disc.

It slammed into the Genestealers, but barely slowed them down.

'Everybody out,' Zelia shouted, ushering everyone into the caves. They ran towards a tunnel on the other side of the cavern.

'Give me the grav-gun,' Talen said as Genestealers poured out of the ship.

'Not yet,' she said, firing a bolt of energy up into the stalactites above their heads. Talen pulled her back as the roof came crashing down on the monsters.

'Let's see them dig their way out of that,' Zelia said, trying to kick over one of the glowing rocks, now twice its natural weight. She shoved the grav-gun back into his hands. 'Come on.'

CHAPTER EIGHTEEN

A Final Escape

'Do you have my lume-rod?' Zelia asked as they hurried through the dark tunnels.

'Yeah, might have dropped that,' Talen admitted. 'Sorry.'

'I just wish we had a map of the caves,' Mekki said.

Talen stopped suddenly. 'We don't need one. Can you feel that?'

Zelia frowned at him. 'Feel what?'

'A breeze.' He licked his finger and held it in front of him. 'Definitely a breeze. This way.'

Talen took the lead, following the draught, years of exploring the tunnels beneath Rhal Rata finally paying off.

'Look,' he said, 'there's a light ahead.'

'Reckon that's where you fell into the sinkhole?' Zelia asked.

'If not, it might be another way out.' They charged into a familiar cavern. 'Yes. We came through here earlier, when we escaped the Ambull.' Talen pointed at an exit to the left of them. 'The pit is this way.'

He ploughed on, the light intensifying, only to nearly barrel straight into a large, hulking figure.

The Ambull bellowed in rage, and Talen stopped so fast that the others slammed into him. Up close, the monster's injuries were clear to see. The claw marks scored into its chest were red raw and its mandibles cracked, but even in its ravaged condition, the thing was still terrifying.

Talen raised the grav-gun and pressed the trigger button, but the beamer just clicked. He tried it again, but nothing happened.

'We must have drained the power pack.'

'That's the least of our problems,'
Zelia told him.

Talen turned and saw Scarface
blocking their escape route. The
Genestealer looked in a worse state
than the Ambull, but it could still
rip them limb from limb. They were
trapped.

Scarface pounced, but was blocked as
the Ambull barged past the children to
pile head first into the Genestealer's
chest. The alien was crushed against

the wall, its claws raking the Ambull's carapace. The two monsters rolled to the ground, locked in a titanic battle, all thought of the children forgotten.

'Down here!' Talen yelled, following the light.

'This is it,' Zelia said, as they came out into a familiar cavern. 'This is where we found you.'

Talen pointed up at the snapped cable still hanging from the canopy high above.

'Yeah, but how are we going to get out this time? I don't fancy taking on whoever wins that fight.'

Fleapit held out a hand.

Talen shrugged at the ape. 'What?'

'I think he wants the grav-gun,' Mekki told him.

'But it's out of juice,' Talen said, handing it over.

The Jokaero started reconfiguring the beamer, the weapon emitting a high-pitched whine.

Mekki's eyes went wide as he realised

what the alien was doing. 'Grab hold of Flegan-Pala.'

'Why?' Talen asked.

'Remember what I did with the force field?' Mekki replied, as the alien turned the beamer inside out.

'You reversed it...' Talen began, before he, too, worked out what was about to happen.

He threw his arms around the alien as a blue bubble blossomed from the transformed grav-gun. Talen closed his eyes, half expecting to be crushed into the ground. Instead, they floated up from the cavern floor, suddenly lighter than air.

'Have I ever mentioned I hate heights?' he wailed as they shot up out of the hole and kept on going, floating towards the top of the canopy.

'Shouldn't we be stopping?' Zelia asked, as they sailed past the mushroom caps.

Fleapit was frantically trying to adjust the grav-gun. With a grunt, he looked up at Mekki and shrugged.

'He cannot stop it,' the Martian shouted. 'Jump!'

The children threw themselves from Fleapit, dropping down onto the nearest giant mushroom. Talen bounced on the spongy cap and started rolling towards the edge. He scrambled to stop himself, his fingers digging into the mushroom's flesh.

His legs went over the edge, but before he could fall, a hairy hand slammed down over his wrist, anchoring him in place.

Talen looked down, his head spinning as he saw the ground far, far below. With a snort, Fleapit hoisted him back up to safety.

'You know, you're not that bad for an oversized hairball,' Talen gasped, rolling onto his back.

High above them, the grav-gun continued floating into the clouds. Talen wondered if it would stop before it drifted out of the atmosphere.

'So,' Mekki said, peering over the edge, 'how are we going to get down?'

'Climb?' Zelia suggested.

'No,' Talen said firmly. 'No way. Not me.'

Zelia looked at him. 'Even if the Ambull stops Scarface, it won't be long before the rest of the Genestealers dig themselves out of those rocks. You want them to climb up here and get you?'

Talen sighed. Was this what their life was going to be like now, lurching from one crisis to another? He could see their camp in the distance, the distress beacon stretching high above the domed shelter. Talen didn't want to think about the state they would find it in. Even if Fleapit could repair the damage caused by Scarface, how would they protect it from the rest of the Genestealers?

His hand went to his belt, where his pouch should be.

Zelia was right. As usual.

'Fine,' he said, giving in to the

inevitable and clambering back to his feet. 'The sooner we start, the sooner we can tumble to our doom. Are you coming?'

When there was no answer, Talen turned to find the others staring into the sky.

'Now what are you lot gawping at?' he asked, as a sound like thunder filled the air.

He looked up to see a spaceship swooping towards them. At first, Talen thought the triangular craft was going to slice through the forest like an arrowhead. He even considered leaping from the canopy – anything to avoid the laser cannons that bristled on the spaceship's scarlet hull.

But the ship didn't carve a path through the trees or open fire. Instead, retrorockets fired beneath its long angular wings, and it hung in front of them like a bird of prey ready to strike.

'I'm guessing that's not your mum?'

Talen asked, as they stared into the darkened cockpit.

'No,' Zelia said, shaking her head.

'Then whose ship is it?' he asked.

'I think we are about to find out,' Mekki said as a ramp lowered onto the mushroom cap.

As the children huddled together, a tall figure swept down the ramp to meet them...

GALACTIC COMPENDIUM

PART TWO

JOKAERO

The Jokaero may
look like apes from
Terra's ancient past,
but appearances
can be deceiving.
These orange-furred
aliens are incredibly
intelligent, with a
natural affinity for
technology and machinery. Give them a
pile of seemingly useless junk and they
can craft intricate, and often deadly,
weapons.

Although their origins are lost in the mists of time, the simian-like creatures are prized throughout the Imperium. Many are recruited to assist the Inquisition, while others are sold into slavery, passing from master to master for generations. Despite only being able to communicate by a series of grunts and whoops, the Jokaero possess an unparalleled understanding of the universe. They are able to tap into unseen power currents that run through the galaxy and can create micro-dimensions capable of storing vast quantities of mechanical parts.

JOKAERO CONSTRUCTS

Digi-Weapons
The Jokaero are masters of miniaturisation, able to squeeze powerful weapons into tiny objects such as rings. These can include laser blasters, flamethrowers and even darts.

Unfortunately, these minute weapons often take a while to recharge after use.

Spy-Flies
Resembling buzzing insects, these crystalline devices swarm into enemy territory and transmit information back to base. They can operate across a distance of twenty kilometres and can even deliver a three-dimensional holographic image of the enemy camp.

Defence Orb
One of the most powerful weapons ever devised, defence orbs contain a fragment of a star. When detonated, a single orb  can wipe out all life for miles around. Luckily, very few Jokaero have mastered the construction of these portable solar flares.

GENESTEALERS

Some of the
deadliest
creatures in
the universe,
Genestealers
swarm across the
galaxy controlled
by a shared hive
mind. They have
two sets of arms.
The first is almost human, while the
second ends in vicious claws that can
slice through metal.

TYPES OF PLANETS IN THE IMPERIUM

Agri Worlds –
Covered in farmland,
Agri Worlds are
planets that have
been completely given
over to the production
of food, which is
mainly shipped to
neighbouring Hive Worlds.

Armoury Worlds – Planets that
only exist to store weapons for the
Emperor's eternal war against the
aliens that threaten the Imperium.

Death Worlds – Their ominous name
says it all. These are planets covered
in carnivorous plants and dangerous
predators. They are
almost impossible
to colonise, but that
doesn't stop people
trying.

Desert Worlds – Arid, sand-covered globes. Many of the Imperium's Desert Worlds were once covered in lush vegetation, before decades of relentless warfare reduced them to barren husks.

Forge Worlds –
Planets dedicated to the creation of machinery and weapons. Highly polluted, these worlds are covered in manufactoria, spewing toxic fumes into their poisoned atmospheres. In many cases, even the planet's oceans have been boiled away to make room for more manufactoria.

Hive Worlds –
Densely populated
planets that provide
much of the
workforce for the
Imperium. Citizens
live in gigantic
towers that stretch

high into the planet's atmosphere.

Ice Worlds – Planets
entirely covered
in glaciers and
tightly packed snow.
Temperatures rarely
rise above freezing
on these inhospitable
worlds.

Ocean Worlds – A planet completely
covered in water, with little or no
land mass.

Waste Worlds – Planet-wide dumping
grounds, Waste Worlds are used to
store rubbish and toxic material
transported from all across the
Imperium.

Xenos Worlds – The official name for a planet outside the Imperium of Man, often the home world of an intelligent alien species.

ZELIA'S OMNISCOPE

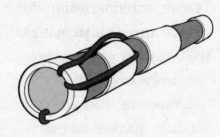

Zelia's Omniscope is a device that was discovered by her mother on the Desert World of Mannia-4. The device can be extended to act as a telescope, or retracted to become a microscope or medi-scanner. Its built-in cogitator contains a vast database accessed by spoken instructions. As a joke, Elise Lor had Mekki program the computer's speech synthesiser with her own voice print. Now, it is Zelia's only link to her mother.

SERVO-SPRITES

Tiny human-like robots
created by Mekki to help
on board the *Scriptor*.
These tiny automatons
resemble the faeries of old
Terran legends, complete
with fragile mesh wings.
With sharp probes instead
of fingers, and wide
picter-lenses for eyes,
Mekki's sprites have no intelligence of
their own, but are programmed to be
fiercely loyal to their master.

DID YOU KNOW?

Inventing new devices is prohibited
throughout the Imperium by order of
the Emperor himself.

WHAT DO YOU DO IF YOU STUMBLE INTO AN AMBULL NEST?

Basically, run.
Ambulls are huge
aliens encased in
thick, insect-like
armour. Usually
found underground
on Desert Worlds,
these hulking
brutes can
tunnel through
solid rock with
their razor-sharp claws. Able to see
in the dark, Ambulls create complex
subterranean burrows and eat most
things they encounter, including metal!
They live in small family groups, and
will do anything to protect their young.

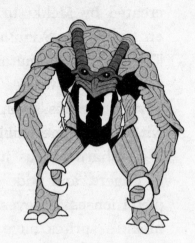

DID YOU KNOW?
Some criminals have tried to train
Ambulls as guards. It never goes
well!

VOX-CASTER

A Vox-Caster
is an Imperial
communication device
that transmits via
radio waves. Most
vox-casters are short
range, and susceptible
to interference.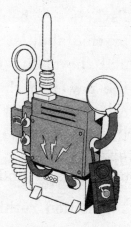
For this reason,
they're unsuitable for interplanetary
communication.

   In fact, there's only one way to
communicate from planet to planet –
telepathy! The Imperium employs
legions of psykers known as Astropaths
to transmit and receive messages across
their vast empire. Even then the results
are often unreliable, with most planets
cut off from their galactic neighbours.

DID YOU KNOW?

Psykers are beings who have special psychic abilities such as telepathy and the ability to move objects with the power of their minds. Some can also control fire or predict the future. On the whole, humans distrust psykers, who are seen as a threat to the Imperium. The Inquisition ruthlessly hunts them down, either press-ganging them into service or destroying them without mercy.

DID YOU KNOW?

Chaos is the Imperium's name for the Dark Powers and armies that exist within the warp. They are feared throughout the galaxy, their followers ruthlessly hunted and destroyed.

ABOUT THE AUTHOR

Cavan Scott has written for such popular franchises as *Star Wars, Doctor Who, Judge Dredd. LEGO DC Super Heroes, Penguins of Madagascar, Adventure Time* and many, many more. The writer of a number of novellas and short stories set within the *Warhammer 40,000* universe, including the *Warhammer Adventures: Warped Galaxies* series, Cavan became a UK number one bestseller with his 2016 World Book Day title, *Star Wars: Adventures in Wild Space – The Escape*. Find him online at www.cavanscott.com.

ABOUT THE ARTISTS

Cole Marchetti is an illustrator and concept artist from California. When he isn't sitting in front of the computer, he enjoys hiking and plein air painting. This is his first project working with Games Workshop.

Magnus Norén is a freelance illustrator and concept artist living in Sweden. His favourite subjects are fantasy and mythology, and when he isn't drawing or painting, he likes to read, watch movies and play computer games with his girlfriend.

WARPED GALAXIES

An Extract from book three
Secrets of the Tau
by Cavan Scott
(out August 2019)

The monsters were coming. They
were scrambling up the towering
mushroom-trees, their claws slicing
into the mottled trunks. Zelia didn't
know which way to run. She had
scuttling aliens to the back of her
and a heavily armed spaceship to
the front. A woman stood on the
gangplank, her longcoat billowing in
the wind. She wore a curved sword
in a scabbard, a beamer slung low on
her waist. Her fingers were covered
with rings, and her long brown hair

was swept back beneath a tri-cornered hat.

'Who are you?' Zelia asked as the woman stared at them incredulously.

'Who cares?' Talen snapped at her, before turning to the newcomer.
'We're about to be lunch. There are Genestealers on their way... Lots of Genestealers.'

'So it would appear,' the woman said as one of the creatures scrambled into view. It hissed, its long tongue tasting the air. 'Get on the ship.'

Talen was right – introductions could wait.

'Don't look at its eyes,' the woman shouted, running back up the gangplank. She snatched up her beamer and fired, the bolt hitting the Genestealer in the chest. It was thrown over the edge, its howl echoing through the forest.

The danger wasn't over. The rest of the pack were closing in fast.

'Move,' the woman commanded,

stepping aside so the children could race up the boarding ramp.

'You don't have to tell us twice,' Talen said, pelting up the gangplank, Zelia and Mekki following close behind. Fleapit brought up the rear, running on all fours.

All the time, the woman was firing, picking off Genestealers as they scrabbled over the edge. She only paused as Fleapit scampered past.

'Is that a...?' she began, before deciding that conversation was best left for now. 'Never mind.'

She turned to bolt up the ramp, the monsters at her heels.

Talen looked around, spotting a barrel near the wall. It clanged as he yanked it over on its side and kicked it down the gangplank. It rolled down the ramp, taking the Genestealers with it.

'Clever boy,' the woman said, slapping a control at the top of the slope. The ramp swung up, shutting the monsters out. 'Although next time try not to waste a barrel of promethium, eh?'

'You'd rather I let them in?' Talen snapped back.

'Oh, I like you.' She turned and sprinted through the ship. 'But that won't keep them out for long. Come on.'

The children followed her, chasing through arched corridors to emerge onto a pristine flight deck.

Zelia was impressed. Her mother's ship, the *Scriptor*, was a ramshackle affair, held together by rust and clutter. In contrast, the woman's flight deck was spotless, gleaming cogitator terminals edged with shining brass. The deck plates were polished and the lume-globes bright. Even the seats were covered in the finest grox-leather.

It was perfect, except for one small detail.

'Where are your crew?' Zelia asked. A ship this size should have been full of people, each station on the flight deck manned. Instead, the only other soul − if you could call it that − was a mindless servitor standing dumbly in the corner. The woman didn't even acknowledge its presence, which wasn't surprising. According to official records, servitors were vat-grown clones, their limbs replaced by cybernetic parts. Barely more than walking lumps of muscle, they were used for manual labour all across the Imperium and always gave Zelia the creeps. There was something about their eyes... so dull and lifeless. And of course there were the rumours of what... or rather *who*... they *really* were.

Striding across the deck, the woman threw her hat through the air. It landed on the servitor's chrome-plated head. The cyborg didn't even flinch.

She dropped behind the flight controls and primed the engines. The deck plates trembled as the plasma drives kicked in, although the only sound was the rasp of claws trying to slice through the ceramite hull.

'Hold on to something,' the woman barked as she grabbed the yoke and pulled back. Zelia stumbled as the ship zoomed up from the mushroom forest. She would have ended up on her back if Talen hadn't reached out to steady her.

The ganger's grip tightened as a Genestealer appeared at the top of the viewport. It was clinging on to the hull as the voidship climbed through the planet's thin atmosphere, its claws scraping against the armourglass.

'If you've scratched my ship...' the woman told the creature, slamming the yoke to the left. The ship banked sharply sending the children tumbling to the deck.

By the time Zelia looked up, the Genestealer was gone, thrown clear by the sudden movement. The woman levelled the ship, before calling over to Mekki.

'You. Tech-Head. Can you operate cameras?'

A flash of irritation passed over Mekki's pale face. 'Of course I can.'

The woman slapped the co-pilot seat beside her. 'Then check to see if any Tyranids are still along for the ride.'

'Tyranids?' Zelia asked.

'The Genestealers,' the woman replied as Mekki slipped into the seat. 'They're a Tyranid sub-species.' Her eyes narrowed as she glanced back at Zelia. 'Don't you kids know anything?'

Zelia grabbed a chair to steady herself. 'We could start with who you are?'

The woman didn't look up from her dashboard, the ship shuddering as they broke free of the atmosphere. 'I'm the person who just saved you from a fate worse than death.'

'What's worse than death?' Talen asked.

'When it comes to Genestealers, you don't want to know.'

She turned back to her controls, which only infuriated Zelia all the more.

'Well?' she demanded.

The woman rolled her eyes. 'Fine. I'm Captain Harleen Amity and this is the *Profiteer*. Better?'

Zelia bristled at the tone, but forced herself to remain civil. 'I'm Zelia, this is Talen and your new co-pilot is Mekki.'

'Pleased to make your acquaintance,' Amity replied. 'How are we doing with those cameras, Mekki?'

The Martian reported that the hull was clear of Genestealers, and the raucous bellow of the engines lowered in pitch to a steady thrum. Ahead of them, the planet's atmosphere had given way to a starfield. They were back in space.

Amity thanked him, and turned towards Fleapit, who was walking around the flight deck, inquisitive eyes examining each and every station.

'And what about your furry friend?'

'That's Fleapit,' Talen said, only to be corrected by Mekki.

'Flegan-Pala,' the Martian said, using their companion's real name.

'A Jokaero,' Amity said, staring at Fleapit's orange back. 'Never seen one in the flesh. Where did you buy him?'

Fleapit turned and bared his teeth at her.

'We didn't,' Zelia said hurriedly. 'He's a survivor, like us.'

'A survivor of what?'

Zelia told the captain everything, how she and her mother had been excavating a dig on Targian when the hive world had been attacked and destroyed by invading Necrons. Zelia and the others had barely escaped with their lives.

'And you landed on a planet infested with Genestealers?' Amity whistled. 'Necrons *and* Tyranids. You must be tougher than you look. What did you say the hive world was called?'

'Targian,' Zelia repeated.

Amity shook her head. 'Can't say I've heard of it.'

She tapped one of the rings on her fingers and the flight deck lights dimmed. The air fizzed as pinpricks of light appeared around them.

'Are those stars?' Talen asked, his eyes wide.

'Top marks,' Amity replied, swatting Mekki's servo-sprite out of her way. 'This is a star map of the Imperium. Every dot represents a star system.'

She strolled through the hololith, searching every star system in turn. 'Targian... Targian... No, I can't see it.'

'It is near the Adrantis Nebula,' Mekki informed her.

Amity's eyebrows shot up. 'In the Segmentum Pacificus? But that's on the other side of the Imperium.' She twisted the ring around her finger and the holo-map zoomed in to one particular system.

'That's it,' Zelia said, recognising the fourth planet from the sun. 'That's Targian.'

'But it can't be,' Amity insisted. 'You say you escaped in a life-pod.'

Talen nodded. 'Yeah. We were thrown clear when the refugee ship made the leap into the...' He searched for the right word, his cheeks flushing as he struggled to remember.

'Into the warp?' Amity prompted.

He shifted, embarrassed. 'Yeah.'

'Talen hasn't travelled much,' Zelia cut in, trying to save the ganger's blushes. It didn't work.

'Thanks, Zelia,' he hissed.

Amity didn't seem to notice. She was shaking her head in amazement. 'You kids must have the luck of the Emperor.'

'What do you mean?' Mekki asked, rising from his seat.

Amity twisted her ring and the star chart pulled out to show the entirety of the Imperium of Mankind, over a million planets filling the bridge.

Amity strode over to a pulsing red dot near the rear of the flight deck. 'This is Targian...' she said, before pointing to a flashing yellow light by the viewport. 'And that's where I found you. A planetoid so remote it hasn't even got a name.'

A holographic line traced from one planet to the other, bisecting the map of the galaxy.

Zelia felt sick. 'But that's...'

'Impossible?' The captain walked the length of the flight deck. 'You're not joking. Somehow, you ended up in the Ultima Segmentum, travelling trillions of light years in a single bound.'